Fabrications

First published in Oxford in 2018 by

Ramsten Publishing
Oxford, United Kingdom
www.ramstenpublishing.com

ramstenpublishing@gmail.com

Cover design by www.davidmunozart.com © 2018

Typeset in Alex Brush © 2011 TypeSETit, LLC and Baskerville by Anna Ramsten, Oxford.

ISBN (Paperback): 978-1-9164715-0-4
ISBN (eBook, ePUB): 978-1-9164715-1-1
ISBN (eBook, Kindle): 978-1-9164715-2-8

This book's printing location may be found on the last page.

A CIP catalogue record for this book is available from the British Library.

If you enjoyed this book, please let the author know by sending the publisher an email.

Fabrications

Amanda Goransson

Ramsten Publishing

To my daughter, Naomi. Your tenacity, love for adventure and determination to face your fears inspire me. I am so proud to be your mother. May you and the generation you represent always know how loved and special you are.

Day 1

Dear Diary,

I need to tell you what happened yesterday. The monthly try-outs to become a Reachable were taking place and I decided that now was my chance.

After completing a number of tests regarding my appearance, weight, posture and communication skills, it was time for the final assessment.

I walked onto the stage. The spotlights blinded me. As I stood there facing the judges, my legs shaking and my breathing agitated, I began to feel that I had made a terrible mistake.

Time stood still as the judges looked me up and down with their unforgiving stares. Frowns appeared on their foreheads, their mouths tensed up. Their eyes narrowed into slits and it seemed as if a black cloud was forming over their heads. I sensed anger, something was wrong.

I heard whispers and laughing from the left corner of the room. As I looked over I saw the other contestants' faces filled with mockery and scorn. It hurt to see them laugh at me when all I wanted was to be like them. They were stunning. Breathtakingly beautiful in their long dresses, flawless make-up and perfect bodies. Each one of them had auditioned before me and been accepted into the world of the Reachables. My whole life I had longed to be one of them.

Suddenly, I heard my name being called and my focus was pulled back to the judges.

'Abisha, we must inform you that you have failed. You do not live up to any of the requirements of becoming a Reachable. Your speech was incoherent, your posture laughable, your body shape disgraceful and as for your face, are you trying to humiliate us by trying out? Is this some kind of joke? We have neither the time nor the energy to deal with people like you. Have you forgotten what you have been taught in school? You must know our requirements by now: complete perfection, no wrinkle or blemish. And as for your weight, do you really think we would even consider allowing someone who is … you know the word, *fat*, into our group? Are you not aware that we can report you to the Mirror? You are certainly playing with fire, young lady. You have brought great shame over yourself and over our try-outs. Make sure to stay out of our way and never, and I mean *never*, try out again.'

The force of his harsh words rushed towards me like a hurricane and caused me to take a step backwards. As I stood there, exposed to their judgement, my heart sank and my hopes crumbled. I felt like a birthday balloon that someone had forgotten to tie up, with all my air seeping out, leaving a crumpled up piece of rubber – empty, unwanted and useless. I knew that I had to get out of there as soon as possible.

I turned to walk away, but the floor beneath me turned blurry as tears welled up in my eyes and I struggled to put one foot in front of the other. The sound of the jury's mocking laughter followed me far into the hallway. I felt humiliated. To think that I had a chance amongst the elite, the chosen few?

Once I made it out of the building I ran all the way home, covered in a blanket of shame. When I came home, I kicked off my shoes and went straight up to my room without even saying hello to my aunt. I threw myself on my bed and pulled the covers over my head. I lay there for hours, weeping as the events of the day replayed in my mind. I hate myself and I'm so angry that I listened to that voice in my dream. All my life I've heard about these try-outs and secretly longed to take part of them, but had never believed I would, or could, try out myself. Not until I heard that voice calling me in my dreams.

It all started five weeks ago. I was lying in my bed, asleep, when I heard a voice. It was a man's voice and he said,

'Abisha, you are beautiful. You are special. Believe in yourself and rise up'.

I heard the words three times and then the voice was gone. Just a few simple words, but I could not shake them. The tone of his voice was like nothing I had ever heard before. A sound from another world, another time. It was comforting and challenging at the same time, powerful, yet meek, mysterious, yet simple, gentle, yet persuasive.

Over the next few weeks the dream came to me repeatedly, communicating the same message. Affirming me that I was beautiful. I was left stunned every time. Never had anyone said these things to me. For as long as I can remember, I've been taught to never believe that I could become anything. At school the message communicated is clear: *Becoming a Reachable is something reserved for the chosen few.* But the voice that had come to me in the night had challenged these statements, and evoked something deep within me – hope. It was hope that had inspired me to try out, but now that hope had left me with broken dreams. Even worse, I'm sure the Agents of the Mirror will be observing me now, perhaps even follow me.

I look into my bedroom mirror and the image staring back at me makes me want to cry. It is true what they said about me, I am fat and ugly. The voice was lying. There is nothing beautiful about me. Nothing special. I hate myself. I hate being fat. I don't deserve to live in this world. I'm overwhelmed and need a place where I can let out all the turmoil and pain inside of me.

That's where you come into the picture. I've decided to keep a diary, somewhere I can express my thoughts and feelings. I really hope that you won't judge me, hate me or accuse me. If you only knew the great risk that I'm taking. If I were to be found out ... I tremble to imagine what they would do to me.

Day 2

Dear Diary,

I have a plan. After what happened this weekend, I decided to do something about being fat. Dieting is the way forward for me and I'm ignoring the gnawing hunger pangs in my stomach. I've decided to embrace them as a friend. In fact, they bring me comfort.

Today, I felt good about myself as I walked along the lunch line and passed by the chips, the meat and the bread. I saw the coated doughnuts that I love, but refused to allow myself to have any. Discipline. That's what my body needs now and I don't care how much it screams out in protest. Carrots and apples, are all I allowed myself to eat.

My friend Sandy's blue eyes filled with disbelief when I walked past my favourite pie. She cried out,

'Abisha, what's wrong with you? You love that pie. Aren't you going to have some? Are you feeling sick or something?'

'I don't want to talk about it, Sandy.' I told her, 'I don't need all that stuff anymore. That was the old me. I've made some new decisions in my life, that's all.'

Sandy is a kind friend and I don't mean to hurt her, but I have a feeling that if I tell her everything, she may want to stop me. I don't want to face her questions. This decision isn't something that I want anyone else to be involved in. It's my life and my body and I don't need people telling me what to do or what to eat.

The same goes for my aunt. I only picked at the lasagne she prepared tonight. We sat at the dinner table together. She put down her knife and fork and, raising her eyebrows, said,

'You are not eating much tonight, Abisha.'

I mumbled something about not feeling well and asked to be excused. She let me go and I was relieved when I made it back to the safety of my room. What does she know, anyway? She wants to force food into me, but it won't help, only harm me.

It's a good plan I have, Dairy. No more listening to voices in dreams for me. I can never be a Reachable, but I can be thin.

On a brighter note, all seems to be going well after my little episode with the try-outs and I haven't noticed anyone following me. Well, as long as you don't count what I saw on my way home from school today, but I'm sure it was nothing.

I was about five minutes' walk from school when I thought I saw one of the Mirror's Agents out of the corner of my eye. I turned to look, but all that was there was a cat. I shuddered when I saw it. It may seem silly, being scared of a cat, but it was an unusual one. It had deep green eyes that were so intense that as I looked into them they pierced deep into my soul. It shook me up a little. When I was three years old, a cat scratched my face, leaving a long, thin scar on my right cheek. Since then, I haven't been a great fan of them and I'm sure this one could feel that. I've never heard that they've used cats before, to do their spying I mean. No, I'm sure it was nothing and that I'm safe.

Day 3

My feelings overwhelm me. The shame, the hate, the anger, hopelessness – all of them erupt like a tidal wave inside of me and I'm drowning in them. Jill's words hurt me today and they still echo inside of my head. *Hi fatty, I thought blubber belonged only on a whale's back and not on humans.*

Sandy said I shouldn't care, shouldn't listen to what Jill said. She said it doesn't matter how much the others laugh at me and that I shouldn't bother about what others think.

'You know that it's not true, Abisha.' she pleaded, 'Don't listen, you are—'

'Don't say it!' I had interrupted her. 'Don't say those words, not now. Don't try to pretend. You know that I don't have a chance. I'm a Shadow Dweller, that is my birthright. I can never be … never!'

After that everything went into a downward spiral. Yesterday's feelings of control unravelled like the pair of socks I tried to knit last year. Each stitch slid off the needle, removing all the hard work I had put into it until all that was left was a pile of twisted, shapeless wool.

Waves of self-hate wash over me. My thoughts are filled with darkness. All I can think is that I am nothing, nothing but fat and ugly. I have no right to live in this world, people like me should be punished.

Day 4

I don't want to go to school today. I knocked my alarm clock onto the floor when it rang earlier. It kept on ringing, reminding me that I cannot escape life, and eventually I found the strength to turn it off. I feel nauseous, hunger mixed with fear doesn't make a great cocktail.

I don't want to face everyone at school again. I'm so ashamed of my body and I have nothing pretty to wear. But what's worse, facing them or the Mirror finding out? All school attendance is recorded and I can't risk bringing any more attention to myself right now. I'll have to go, even though I'm late now. I'll wear my blue, faded dress that Sandy gave me for my birthday last year. It's baggy and should hide my body. I'll make up some excuse about my alarm not going off.

Day 5

I like having you to talk to, Diary. It really feels as if you're listening to me. We have to be careful though, very careful. I'm afraid there is no getting around it. I'm being followed.

Today, I decided to take the scenic route home from school, by the mountains. I wanted to avoid the other students. I can't bear them teasing me. I longed to see the flowers and to breathe in some fresh air.

The mountains have always been a special place for me. As a child, I often looked out of my bedroom window up at the summit of Prospect Mountain. It is covered with snow all year round and has that magical, otherworldly look about it. I used to imagine how I would climb to the top, then shout out my name and hear it echo throughout the valley.

I've never actually climbed to the top, we are only allowed halfway up the mountain. There is a grass area where picnics are allowed, but no one has ever been permitted further than that. Not since the Mirror took over Genville anyway. The mountains are a place of refuge for me, and more than anything else, somewhere I can feel free to have my own thoughts.

Being up in the mountains reminds me of the rumours that are occasionally whispered in the valley. Rumours of another dimension beyond what we know, a world in which the Mirror has no control. Usually, I ignore such nonsense, and my aunt absolutely forbids me to mention such ideas. But when I look up to them, I sometimes wonder …

Today was one of those perfect days. The sun, undefeated by the clouds and the mountain peak clearly visible. The blue sky painted a heavenly picture and spoke of hope and freedom. I sat on my favourite piece of grass gazing upwards when suddenly I saw them. I know that I was not imagining it, although I wish I was. I saw them, with my own eyes.

They are after me. At first I thought there was only one, but then I saw that there were three of them. That is *really* bad news. I've heard talk about them sending two, but three, that is almost unheard of. It must mean that they see me as a real threat. I just can't understand why. I mean, I know I tried out for the Reachables, but others have done that before, failed and still survived. Been left alone I mean.

I know they let me see them in order to scare me. That's their way. Otherwise they prefer to remain hidden and observe at a distance. They didn't come very close, but close enough for me to see their claws. They were razor-sharp and I know I wouldn't stand a chance. I stood petrified for what seemed like hours until I sensed that they had left.

As I walked home in shock, the only conclusions that I could come to were:

1. These things are not a human
2. The Mirror must have sent them

These Creatures are the sort of things we would whisper about in the school playground when we were younger. The parents in the valley always denied their existence and as for our teachers, we were forbidden to even ask about them. *Taboo* is what Sandy calls it. That is another part of our valley life which is unnerving. Whenever we try to question anything, we are silenced and ridiculed. The Mirror has always tried to hush up any stories about the Creatures' existence.

'Just nonsense, made up by over-imaginative children or mad adults,' are some of the explanations they've given.

Something tells me that there is so much more than we understand or are allowed to know about. Today was my first contact with the Creatures and there is no doubt in my mind, they are real and their message is clear: *Beware, we are watching you.*

I feel quite shaken. The Mirror has its ways of finding things out. It has its spies and its methods. I'm going to have to be smarter, more careful.

Day 6

Life feels much more positive today. I think maybe I was imagining the whole thing, about being followed. I've always been a little dramatic, or so they've always told me. Too over-sensitive, too much of a thinker, too intense and they are probably right. Three messengers following me? Little me? I must be making it up. Of course I must.

It is going well with my diet, anyway. I'm learning to resist the cries from my stomach and the rumbling is becoming a part of my daily life. I felt a surge of power as I walked past Jill in the lunch line today. She may have compared me to a whale, but I saw how much she ate today. She's always been the type of person who avoids the pies, the potatoes and the bread. Today when she took her salad, I took a smaller one and I didn't allow myself to have the apple that she took for dessert. Just one little salad, I even left the chicken out. I'll show her who can be disciplined.

I was so busy comparing what I ate with everyone else in the room that I didn't have time to talk to Sandy. I could tell that she was hurt because she wasn't smiling, and Sandy is one of the few people in the valley who's always smiling. We usually talk at lunchtime but I'm not sure I have time for friends right now. I've got so much to think about and I'm scared too. I don't want to tell her about the things that have been happening recently. What would she think about me? Perhaps she'll tell someone? Maybe she's one of the Mirror's spies? No, it's better to keep everything inside and not trust anyone. At least I have you to talk to, dear Diary, and that will have to do for now.

School was boring today, although we do have a new history teacher. It seems a little strange, because we normally don't change teachers in the middle of the term like this. His name is Mr Sann and he's taking over from Mr Devin, who we have had for three years.

At first glance, Mr Sann looks ordinary enough. Dark brown hair, cut short and slightly balding on the top. But on closer examination there are some striking aspects about him. He is taller than most of the men in the valley and, for a history teacher, he's very muscular. He looks like he could have been a PE teacher, strong and fit.

Another thing that perplexed me was his eyes. They may twinkle, but they also have a fierceness and sternness about them, as if great wisdom and power lie within him. They appear to see far beyond the classroom and the valley. It makes me think of an eagle. I feel different when I listen to Mr Sann. My instinct tells me that I've felt it before. I can't quite identify why exactly, but I like it and I like him.

He started the day by introducing himself,

'Hello class, my name is Mr Sann. I have been sent to you to teach and support you. By studying the past we can gain understanding of our present, and even our future. I hope that we will have many interesting hours together, exploring new and fascinating topics.'

As he spoke I thought I saw him look at me more than the others, but I'm not sure. I seem to be imagining quite a lot recently and I dare not take myself too seriously.

Day 7

Today is Saturday and it's been a hard day. I spent a lot of time looking in my mirror. We have always been taught that mirrors never lie, but I wish they did. I hate the fact that I'm not perfect and the mirrors highlight every part of me that needs to change. My thighs are far too fat. I'm ugly and disgusting.

I wasn't looking in *the* Mirror of course, in case you get confused. No, I'm talking about the mirrors we all have to have in our homes. One in each room. They are also lined up along the streets, outside of every shop, restaurant, office and school. Our valley is saturated with them. We have them everywhere.

A few years ago, the Agents of the Mirror were dispatched to install them in every house. I still remember when they came to put them on the walls. I felt shivers down my spine as I sensed a dark and oppressive atmosphere invade our home with every mirror they put up. The Agents of the Mirror visit regularly to ensure that all mirrors are intact and that they've not been tampered with in any way.

I've never really understood why we need to have them everywhere. They are just sheets of glass, but they seem to have a life of their own and they really affect you. I mean, when you haven't looked in one for a while, you feel so much better. Your mind clears up and you are able to focus on other things.

It's only the Shadow Dwellers who have these mirrors. I've heard rumours that the Reachables have other rules, that they don't have the same mirrors as we do, but I don't know what is true. They live in their own part of Genville and I've never been allowed in there.

We have orders to look into each mirror that we pass and it is punishable by law to just walk by them. Once, when I was 10 years old, I tried to walk past one outside of the bakery without looking into it. I just wanted to see what would happen. Immediately, a sound was heard over a loudspeaker.

'Abisha, go back and look. We saw you walk by. Go back and look into that mirror immediately or the authorities will be sent upon you.'

I was so terrified that I ran back to the mirror and stood there paralysed until, finally, a friend was sent to fetch my aunt who pulled me away from there. She gave me such a long lecture that, afterwards, I wasn't sure who I feared more: her or the Mirror.

There are rumours that some of the older people in the valley remember a time without the mirrors. Many times I've longed to talk to some of these elderly people, to find out for myself. But of course that is impossible, everyone over sixty years of age has been placed in special lodgings. No one is allowed in or out and it is illegal to talk to any of them.

Anyway, spending so much time looking into the mirrors didn't have the best effect on me.

I didn't eat much today, no more than a little salad and fruit. Time just drags on as there is no school to distract me. I thought about going by the mountains again, but then I remembered what happened last time. The peace of the place is ruined for me now. It's not good for me to have so much time on my hands, not good to think too much. I wish I could turn back the clocks to just a few weeks ago, before the dreams, before the try-outs. Life was boring then, but at least it was safe.

My aunt tried to talk to me today and asked me if everything is all right. She seems to have noticed that I'm not eating as I did before. I don't feel like she really cares when she asks. It's as if she wants to control me somehow, keep me in line.

She has always been like that. Controlling, I mean. Sometimes I've had this funny feeling that she's secretly watching me, monitoring my every move.

I refused to answer her questions and managed to divert her attention by mumbling something about homework. If she knew about the try-outs and me being followed, I dread to think what she might do. Lock me in the house for a month, no doubt. But then that would never work, though. The Mirror would notice and wonder why I wasn't at school. Anyway, I hope this day is over soon.

Day 8

I didn't get out of bed until the afternoon today and even then I didn't have much energy.

I thought about calling Sandy. We usually go swimming at the swimming pool on Sundays but I just didn't have the strength today. Sad, because I love to swim. It's one of the few joys I have here in the valley. There is something about diving under water that exhilarates me. I imagine that I'm a dolphin as I dive in and out of the water. Under water I feel as if I'm in another world and for those few moments, as I hold my breath, there is no pain and I'm free.

Sandy and I love to go swimming together and then eat lunch afterwards. But today not even the thought of diving beneath the surface drew me. I'm not sure I could even walk to the pool, let alone swim. I feel weak, tired and hungry.

I've had far too much time alone in the darkness of my thoughts. I'll have to come up with a better plan for next weekend. This is not working.

Day 9

Monday and back to school again, thankfully. The new teacher Mr Sann intrigues me. There is something about him that I recognise, something familiar about his voice.

I've always loved history and had a longing to understand more about the past. There has been very little that I've been able to discover, though. All of our school life is very controlled, especially the history lessons. We have to memorise everything we are taught in class but on no account are we allowed to do any private study.

People say that there was a time when the library was open in the valley. They say it was a place where you could go and read books from the past. Somewhere you could sit and study. Now it is closed up and we are forbidden to enter. I've walked past it a few times but there are armed Reachables guarding it day and night. The little history that we learn is so limited and often I wonder if they are telling us the whole truth. I hardly dare to think these thoughts and I've never shared them with my friends, though I'm sure they must have had the same questions as me.

Mr Sann taught us from the usual textbook today, but when he spoke I found myself mesmerised. I wanted to hear more. When the bell rang for break I was actually disappointed. There is something in the way that he teaches that awakens something in me. I'm not sure what it is but it makes me hungry, not for food but for knowledge.

Hunger … that is something I've struggled with all day. As much as I was interested in what Mr Sann had to say, I found myself struggling to concentrate in my other classes. I've been feeling pretty weak and dizzy lately. My stomach screams at me, rumbling and rumbling, demanding food. It's overwhelming and a constant reminder that I'm empty inside. Today when the lesson was over, I stood up too quickly and had to steady myself against my chair. The whole classroom swayed before my eyes. I caught a glimpse of Mr Sann's face and he appeared to want to reach out and help me, but then something held him back. The next thing I knew everything went black before my eyes. I felt someone grab a hold of me and then I heard Sandy asking me if I was all right. She gave me something to drink and then urged me to follow her to the cafeteria.

'Abisha, you are not eating enough, come on, let's go and sit and eat your favourite snack, it will make you feel better I promise.'

I refused. I don't care how weak I feel, I'm not going to let a few moments of dizziness stop me from my goal. I'm tired of being fat and the only way to change things is to stop eating. It didn't matter how much Sandy protested. I refused to listen to her and all I allowed myself to eat was an apple, that's enough for me.

Who needs food anyway? I certainly don't. It just messes you up and makes you look ugly. My body will just have to learn to bow down to me. I'm not giving it what it wants. It doesn't deserve it.

Day 10

I've always been like this you know, stubborn. Once I've decided something I won't back down, no matter how hard or demanding the task. I guess that is why I was stupid enough to try out for the Reachables. I had an idea, and was determined to follow it through. Never mind, I've learned my lesson now.

There has been a lot of changes in our school recently. First Mr Sann's arrival and today a new guy joined our class. I don't know where he comes from but he looks different. He has blue eyes and golden hair, which is wavy and not at all like the strict style the other guys have. The Mirror controls all of the hairdressers here in the valley. Everyone who wants to be trained as a hairdresser is sent to special training academies run by the Reachables. Of course. Everyone is taught with the same manual, the same cutting techniques. More like a factory if you ask me, because everyone who has their hair cut by them ends up looking the same. Short back and sides for the boys and no longer than 10 inches long for the girls. Anyone caught with a different style is first warned, then fined and finally, they disappear.

I remember once when I was 5 years old, I longed for a change and I begged my aunt to let me. I wanted to have long, flowing hair and had boldly told the hairdresser that I wanted to let my hair grow long. I'll never forget the look of fear in my aunt's eyes as I spoke. She looked around us and in hushed tones said,

'Abisha, Abisha be quiet. You must be quiet now.'

Then, before I could say anything else, she rushed me out of the room and into the car. When she was sure no one was listening she warned me,

'Abisha you must never do that again. This is the way it is here, there is nothing you can do to change it. You are born into the shadows and there are rules to follow, no exceptions, especially not for you.'

'But auntie,' I pleaded, 'please, please, I know the way that I want to have it. I've seen it in a dream, please—'

'That is enough, Abisha!' she snapped. 'We will never discuss this again. Forget your dreams. They just cause you and me trouble. Shadow Dwellers do not dream.'

But here I go babbling again. Sorry, dear Diary. Somehow, having a safe place to write brings up things from the past for me and uncovers feelings that have been lying around for a while.

Back to the guy. What really struck me was the way he handled the usual 'new kid' trick. We have a tradition in our school that when someone new starts, they are subject to our trick on their first day. The goal is to humiliate them and initiate them into the rules of the school. It is stupid and cruel, but everyone knows it's just part of the process. No one does anything to stop it, even the teachers choose to turn a blind eye. Today, some of the students in my class had placed a rope in front of the new guy's desk which they planned to pull up as he walked by, to cause him to lose balance and fall on his face.

Everything went as planned, and as he tripped and fell to the ground the whole class burst into laughter. But two things were different today. The first was our teacher's response. It was during history class and, like I told you, Mr Sann is new. Usually, our teachers laugh along with the rest of us, often the loudest of everyone.

All forms of teasing, bullying and unkindness are encouraged in our school. But Mr Sann did not laugh. Instead, his eyes moistened, his brows furrowed and a look of grief overshadowed his face. His mouth opened and it looked as if he was going to call on something or someone for help.

He must have changed his mind because his facial muscles tightened, his back straightened and I almost felt the draft of wind as he took a deep breath and walked over to the new guy. He pulled him to his feet and placed him on a chair nearby and then, with a gentleness that took my breath away, he wiped the dust off the guy's clothes, ruffled his hair and with a smile announced,

'You're all right, son.'

The others, who had stopped laughing by now, stood back in shock. It was as if the whole room was filled with rays of light and the nastiness of the moment evaporated. What was this new thing? Gentleness, kindness, respect? It was if a fragrance of summer roses had entered the room and filled each corner with its life and passion.

If that was not strange enough, the second astonishing thing was the guy's reaction. He wasn't angry, and he didn't shout out the usual stream of curses that is so common when someone feels threatened here in the valley. He kept his head down, pointed towards the floor, then, as Mr Sann reached out to him, he lifted up his head and looked straight into his eyes. It was impossible to miss the twinge of sadness on both their faces. Once Mr Sann had dusted him off, the guy (I still don't know what his name is) looked around at us and without a trace of anger or sarcasm said,

'I'm so happy that I've come to this class. I know that I'm supposed to be here. I hope to become good friends with you all.'

You should have seen how everyone crawled out of that room in shame.

You can bet it was all we talked about at lunch. *Who was this new guy? Where did he come from? Didn't you feel bad when he looked up at us? Why was Mr Sann so kind?* These were just a few of the questions that bounced around amongst us. Not that I ate any lunch, apart from a few vegetables. I feel stronger today and more determined. The kindness we saw in the classroom affected me though and I was tempted to show myself some love too. I was so close to eating a whole meal, but fortunately I caught myself just in time.

It really helps having you to talk to, Diary, I hope you don't mind all my rantings and ravings? It gets easier every day to talk to you and I notice that I dare to share more and more of my thoughts. I'm so used to keeping everything locked up inside of me, but having you in my life really helps.

Day 11

So many things happened yesterday that I forgot to be afraid or worried about being followed and I nearly, and I mean nearly, forgot about being fat. But that was yesterday and today my shadows have caught up with me again. This morning I was getting ready for school and had made the final check of my clothes. I looked at myself in the mirror and everything came cascading back. Oh, how I loathe all mirrors, especially mine. I know we are not allowed to think or even say that here in the valley, but I just can't help myself. That's how I feel. They tell us that the mirrors are better than any friend we could ever have. They say that the mirrors keep us connected and teach us what is real. We are encouraged to look into them as often as possible, the more the better, but today mine seemed to mock me and highlight everything that is wrong with me.

As I looked at my reflection, it was so obvious that my sweater made my bottom stick out. I hate that! Why can't I have one of those perfect bodies, like one of those dolls I had as a child? You know, the ones that you can dress up with any possible combination and they always look faultless. No bits sticking out anywhere! I weighed myself straight after and I've lost a little weight, but obviously not enough. I wanted to scream out with all the helplessness and rage I felt inside.

That was my morning, but then the day went from bad to worse. I'm pretty sure that they are following me again. I took my usual route home, past the bakery. The smell of freshly baked bread nearly caused me to give up on this whole dieting business. I peered through the window and saw the most delicious doughnuts, the ones where you take your first bite and the jam inside oozes out, electrifying your taste buds. I saw my favourite vanilla buns that are beautifully packaged with a white rose on the top.

I really love this bakery and for some reason I've always felt drawn to it. It represents so much warmth and comfort to me. The strangest thing is that sometimes I have flashbacks of me as a young child, sitting in the bakery with a man. I don't know who he is or what he looks like. I only ever see him from behind in my vision. I'm no more 3 years old and dressed in a beautiful dress with a pattern of pink roses all over it. I seem so happy as I sit there and I look … safe, that's the word, happy and safe. I've always connected the bakery with that memory, which is probably why it is one of the places I go whenever I need comfort.

Today, as I looked at the rows and rows of delicious pastries through the window, I became painfully aware of the emptiness and gnawing inside my stomach. I forgot all about the trauma of the morning and I was close to walking in and giving way to the temptation. Fortunately, I was saved by the mirrors again. Just as I was about to walk in, a reflection of light caught my eye from a mirror outside the shop. I turned to look and one glance at my reflection convinced me. No treats today, not with that backside sticking out like it does! It's clear to me. I'm not to allow myself any form of pleasure, not if I'm to have the perfect body I want.

I walked past the bakery and then continued on towards the store where a group of Reachables were hanging out. I hate the way they look at you whenever you walk by them. They are all dressed the same, red tops and black skirts. They are the only ones who are allowed to have long hair and it is usually styled so well that, even on a windy day, not a single hair blows out of place. Their faces are heavily made-up, and they have thick eyelashes which, on a closer look, I'm sure are false. Their skin is flawless, soft as feathers and never a pimple or a spot. Each one has the perfect hour glass shape. Slim waist, long legs. They are dazzling but their haughty looks mock you and convey a clear message: *Don't ever believe that you can be like us, we are the Reachables and you belong in the shadows.*

A wave of relief flowed over me as I remembered that I had managed to resist the pull of the bakery. I even dared to meet their gaze with a quick look of, *You can't touch me.* They sneered at me in response. Only the trained eye would have seen the sinister exchange of silent dialogue that passed between us. Officially, no Reachable may threaten anyone openly without a cause, but we Shadow Dwellers know the unsanctioned truth.

I sped past them around the corner to my treasured place in the village, the town square. You find the most exquisite fountain there and I love to sit on my special bench and watch it, soaking in the sound of the running water. You can see the water being led up a pipe to the top of this beautiful flower-shaped fountain and then it lets out the water, cascading into the pool beneath. I enjoy the playfulness of the water, its freedom to splash and express itself. When I sit on the bench I imagine that I'm one of those drops of water caught up in the flow, being led forward through the pipes, secure and free.

I was in the middle of such a lovely daydream today, when suddenly I felt it. Icy breathing down my back, causing my spine to tense up like a brick wall. There was a smell of death, putrid and gross. I put my hand over my mouth in an attempt to hold back the shriek of terror that surfaced. I dared not look back as I knew I could not face whatever or whoever was behind me. An eerie voice wheezed out,

'You are being watched. We know where you live and, listen carefully, we know who you are.'

Then, just as quickly as the presence appeared, it left and I was alone with only the sound of the fountain. It no longer brought me any peace. All I've ever known up to this point is being shaken. I'm not safe and I feel totally powerless and afraid. What am I to do? What have I gotten myself into?

Day 12

It struck me last night as I was going to sleep that you must think I lead a very exciting life. So much has happened to me since I started writing to you that you might be wondering what kind of girl I am? I realised that you really don't know much about me and I wanted to clear some things up for you: I AM JUST AN ORDINARY SHADOW GIRL. Up until a few days ago, nothing thrilling had ever happened to me.

My name is Abisha Lova Grayson. Long-winded, I know, and I've no idea what it means. I guess I really should look it up one day. I live with my aunt Sophie in a little apartment, right in the centre of the city of Genville. We live on the sixth floor and I have my own room that I've decorated in different shades of blue. I live alone with my aunt because both my parents are dead. I have no memory of my mother. She died when I was a baby and no one has ever talked with me about her. My father died when I was a young child. I have only vague memories of him. Whenever I've tried to ask what happened to him all I've been told are things like,

'Terrible accident. A real shame. Never could understand how it happened, him being such a careful man'. Then people usually go quiet, look uneasily to the left and right and say,

'We can't say any more now, child. Your father was a great man, but it is forbidden to talk about him in these parts of the valley'.

My aunt never wants to talk about him. She is his younger sister and, supposedly, took me in after my father's death as there was no one else to take care of me. I've heard people say about her, 'She never really recovered from the shock ... not the same woman at all afterwards'.

It seems she was deeply affected by my fathers death. I wouldn't know the difference between before and after. All I know is a distant, broken woman who rarely shows emotion of any sort and who works at a shoe box factory. She has never really understood me or the way I work. We seem to come from two different planets and there have been times when I've seriously questioned if we really are related. The older I get the more I feel that she feels obligated to take care of me but does not really love me. I could never come straight out and ask her for fear that she would be hurt or, even worse, get angry. I guess she must love me. She feeds me, makes sure our house is tidy and that the bills are paid, but I often have this nagging feeling that something is missing. When I was younger I would occasionally find myself longing to sit on her lap and be held, to talk, to laugh, to connect in some way. I've long given up on that hope and accepted that the only communication we have is about meals, tidying and reprimands for talking about my dreams or questioning the Mirror. That was many years ago and I learnt my lesson quickly; that such things are forbidden and punishable.

As for my father, all I have of him is a framed photograph that is kept on a round, wooden table in the hallway. I love to look at it. As a child, I would often sit for hours at a time looking into his face, searching for any kind of message he might communicate to me. He was a very handsome man: rugged skin, piercing dark brown eyes which, as a child, I was convinced sparkled and followed me around the room. His hair was curly and untamed (much like the new guy who has started in my class, when I think about it). He has a look about him that I do not recognise in the people of this town, something deep, mysterious and reassuring. So often I ached to talk to him, to share my deepest feelings, my dreams and my questions with him.

Numerous times, I would go sit in front of his picture, especially when I was sad. It brought me such comfort to look at him, to feel as if he was close. I would talk to him. Tell him all about my life, share what happened at school, my thoughts, my fears, everything. But a few years ago I stopped. I got tired of pouring out my heart to someone who never answered. Even though part of me believed that he had heard me through the years, that he delighted in listening to me, another part of me saw how ridiculous that whole situation was, sitting talking to a glass framed photograph hour after hour, so I gave up.

My aunt had a lot to do with my stopping as well. She never liked me talking to his picture and always looked very nervous whenever I did. Like a scared animal, she would look behind her as if someone was watching us. She even threatened to take the photo away if I didn't stop, so eventually I did. We have kept the picture but I hardly ever look at it anymore. I doubt that my father ever really cared about me. If he had, he would never have left us alone like he did. He seemed to be involved in some big research and they say that's what killed him in the end. Was his work more important than his family, than me? I guess I'll never know. But it hurts to think it was.

Please don't think I'm telling you all of this to make you feel sorry for me, Diary. I'm fine, really I am. I've learnt to survive, to make it in this world. I've trained myself to not need anyone else or to show my feelings to anyone (except Sandy sometimes). That has worked really well up until now. Like I said, I'm just an ordinary girl and, compared to many of the inhabitants of this city, I have a pretty good life. We have never been in trouble with the Mirror before, at least not until now. I have certainly never had anything as dramatic happen to me as being followed. What do you think I should do? Should I tell my aunt? Something tells me that I should keep it hidden from her.

I can feel my energy decreasing. Did I tell you that I nearly fainted again today? I was on my way home from school when everything went fuzzy and then black before my eyes. I feel like I'm fading away. It's getting harder and harder to concentrate at school and at home. My thoughts are scattered and broken. I no longer recognise myself and I find so many questions popping up in my mind. These past few years I've just felt like a robot, functioning on the outside but dead on the inside. Now so many feelings are surfacing inside of me and I don't know how to handle them. I know, I should probably eat a little more but I'm determined – I refuse to be know as *Abisha the fat girl* anymore. No, as I'm trying to tell you, I'm just an ordinary girl who wants to be thin.

Good night, dear Diary!

Day 13

I heard my aunt talking on the telephone today, she spoke in hushed tones and I couldn't make out her words. Something is going on – I'm sure of it. Has she found out that I've been followed? Who is it she's talking to? I didn't think she had any friends. I tried to ask her at the dinner table tonight,

'Who were you talking to earlier, auntie?' I asked her as casually as I could.

'That is none of your business,' she replied firmly. 'You shouldn't eavesdrop on other people's conversations, haven't I taught you that?' Impatiently, she continued, 'Now get on with your dinner. Don't think that I haven't noticed that you aren't eating properly. Eat up your meal now, I'm watching.'

You can bet that I seethed with anger at that point. I hate being told what to do, and especially being made to eat at a time when I just can't. Eating is an area I want to have control over, and here she comes trying to take over. You know what I did, Diary? I'm not proud of it and please don't tell anyone about it. I finished my meal in front of her and then I went to the bathroom and threw it all up. It was disgusting sticking my finger down my throat, feeling the partly digested food bits come up and then have them staring at me from the bottom of the toilet bowl. It was horrible and I didn't feel better afterwards, just very ashamed and worthless. The only good thing was the feeling of emptiness inside of me. My aunt isn't going to make me fat or control how much I eat. Besides, I know that she's hiding something from me.

Day 14

Today is Saturday and no school. After what happened last weekend, I knew I had to have some kind of plan to take my mind off of things and make the time go faster. I know it may sound crazy, but I decided to go to the mountains again. I needed to get away and clear my head. A lot is going on at the moment and I don't understand a thing. There is something about the mountains. Like a magnet, I'm pulled towards them.

I admit I was a little hesitant at first after what happened last time I was there. I kept looking behind me at first to see if anyone was following me but I saw no one. Today felt different somehow, like I was protected and not alone. Not in a scary *you are being followed* type of feeling, but rather a *someone is watching over you* sense. I didn't feel any of the fear of last time, but rather felt as if I was enclosed in a soft, warm blanket.

I climbed and climbed until I couldn't see Genville anymore. A spectacular sky stretched out for miles and miles before me. I was hot and sweaty when I finally reached the halfway point which is as far as we are allowed to climb, but the gentle breeze soon cooled me off. It is much easier to think straight up there. I needed to work through some facts that have been hopping around my mind like marbles in a bag on a roller coaster:

1. My aunt is hiding something
2. I'm being followed by the Creatures and more than one – *bad news!*
3. I'm fat and I'm trying to do something about it

As I was thinking about these things, I heard the most beautiful sound. It was the sound of children singing, a melody like nothing I've ever heard before. We used to sing songs at school in the choir, but the songs we sang were boring, lifeless and dictated by the Mirror. I never enjoyed singing or listening to them. This song, however, was totally different. The children sung as if their hearts depended on it, from a place deep within. There were freedom and joy in their voices and I was swept up in the melody, eager to listen more. Where did the sound come from? Who are these children? Something deep inside of me responded and I wondered if the song was just for me? It was like a coded sound, an emissary from another world. I could not make out the words that they sung exactly, but as I listened to the melody I felt so alive and waves of tension and fear fell off of me. I even forgot to worry about how I look.

As I made my way back down the mountain none of my questions had been answered, but I felt calmer. I wish I could keep this feeling with me forever.

Day 15

I have nothing to write today, except to say that my heart is at peace. The children's song is all I can think about. I even ate a little lunch.

Day 16

I didn't have much to share with you yesterday, dear Diary. Today, however, is another story.

I've discovered the new guy's name. It is Allister. He came to sit next to me during lunch break and seemed interested in getting to know me. He asked me lots of questions, especially about my family. I find it very uncomfortable to talk about such personal things as we very rarely discuss our families with each other around here. It's not that we can't, I guess we just don't, a sort of unwritten rule or something. It was really awkward sitting at the lunch table with him as he kept looking at the tiny salad that I had on my plate.

'Aren't you going to eat more than that?' he asked. 'That doesn't seem like enough to keep your energy up.'

I desperately tried to avoid answering his direct question. I mumbled something like,

'I'm not that hungry today. This is all I want.'

Allister didn't ask in a prying sort of way, more like he was interested, even concerned. Strange. Another weird thing was that the whole class was much calmer today, less disruptive and noisy. Allister appears to have a soothing effect on us. Not everyone likes him though. Gale, who is usually the biggest trouble maker in the class, absolutely hates him. He's made that pretty clear. Today he walked past Allister and pushed him up against the wall. He whispered something into his ear and I know it wasn't good wishes. His whole face contorted with animosity when he spoke. I have never liked Gale, he gives me the creeps and I usually try to avoid having any contact with him.

Allister reacted as calmly as he did when the class tripped him up last week. Without a trace of anger, he shrugged his shoulders and smiled at Gale. Not in a patronising way, or with a *I'm better than you* face, but rather with a *I know who I am and you can't frighten me* look. He walked straight past Gale as if nothing had even happened. I could see the frustration and annoyance on Gale's face. He is not used to being dismissed and certainly not used to not being feared. A healthy new experience for him, if you ask me.

We had another history lesson with Mr Sann today. He really makes the past come to life. I sat captivated throughout his class. He was teaching us about the history of Genville. As he taught, images suddenly flashed before me. I saw our town but it seemed to be from another time, years and years ago. I recognised the streets, the town centre, even my favourite fountain. Everything was familiar, yet different. There were no mirrors anywhere. Where did these images come from? Had my hunger made me start hallucinating? Mr Sann looked frustrated as he taught. At least twice it felt as if he had much more to say and then – just as he was about to – he stopped, hesitated and began to talk about something else. I'm so curious. I want to know more about the past.

All through class I debated whether I should talk to him or not, perhaps tell him about the images. He doesn't scare me as such, but I do feel an enormous respect for him. I noticed that he looked over at Allister more than once during the class. The funny thing is that while I was plucking up my courage to talk to Mr Sann, he asked me to stay behind after class today. At first I was a bit nervous as teachers usually only want to talk to you alone if you've done something wrong and they are going to warn or punish you in some way. But talking to him was not the same. First, he asked me how I was getting on in school and I really felt like he genuinely cared. I answered him uneasily, not at all used to someone being interested in how I feel. Then he did something very unexpected. He went over to the classroom door, locked it and quickly pulled out an old leather book from a green bag that was hidden under his desk. He placed the book in my hands and said,

'This is a gift for you and you are the only one who will be able to decipher it. Look past the obvious and let your instinct lead you into the truth. Take care of it Abisha, look for the message and don't show it to anyone.' He gave me no other explanation except these parting words,

'Go now, child, and take the safe route home.'

I felt rattled and left his classroom with my mind reeling. Message? Safe route? I have no idea what he's talking about. Why on earth did he give it to just me? Why did he think that I'm the only one who can uncover some hidden message? I've never owned a book of my own before. We are not allowed to keep or study books outside of school.

I ran all the way home, didn't even dare to look behind me in case I was being followed. So many weird things have happened to me recently. I feel like I'm in some kind of movie and I have no idea what is going on. I've lived such a boring existence up until now but something tells me that everything is about to change. I feel weak from all the tension and running but I can't wait to read the book.

Day 17

I was up half the night reading that dumb book. I didn't find any coded message and if there is one to find, I seriously doubt that I'm the right person to uncover it. I actually wanted to throw it at the wall at around 2 am. I've hidden it under my bed now and I hope Mr Sann won't ask me any questions about it.

Today was a hard day. I've been feeling weaker and weaker and it was difficult to concentrate in class. The teacher's voice seemed to fade into the background and I struggled to keep my eyes open during biology.

I find myself obsessing about what I eat or don't eat. I go over it in my mind. I think through what I've eaten, adding up the calories and working out if I'm allowed any more that day. I don't allow myself to eat more than five hundred calories a day. I feel very dizzy and weak but this is just the way things have to be now. Do you think I should eat an apple more tomorrow, to help with the dizzy spells? Or will it just make me fat? I think I'll play it safe and skip it.

My thoughts are becoming obsessive and I struggle to control them. Somehow I feel that I'm losing my grip over this whole dieting thing. It all started as a way of bringing some order into my life, but now it seems to be taking on a life of its own that soon I won't be able to manage. I did notice that my jeans were not as tight today, so there is some reward.

There is one problem though; I can hardly look in the mirror anymore. It really messes me up and this morning I actually scared myself. I looked in the mirror, as I usually do before going to school, but the eyes that looked back at me did not seem to be my own.

They were filled with intense hatred and loathing. I was terrified. What is happening to me? It feels like there is a ticking bomb inside of me and that, anytime now, it's going to explode. I feel so messed up. Should someone as ugly and fat as me be allowed to live? I'm not sure. I know that we are supposed to look in the mirror at least ten times a day, but after this morning I dread coming anywhere close to one.

Things did not get any better when I arrived at school. It was one of those days when we had to read the hand-outs from the Reachables. Hand-outs are sent out weekly and they are meant to remind the rest of us, the Shadow Dwellers, what we should aim for. Cruel, really, because they know we can never be like them. Every boy and girl in the valley is ordered to look through them page by page. We are monitored, as some have been caught trying to skip a page. I wish I could every time. I hate looking at them. There are countless images of Reachables, all perfectly beautiful and faultless. There is not an ounce of fat showing on their bodies, nor a blemish or line on their faces. We have to spend the whole of our morning break looking at the images and although we are not allowed to discuss what we have seen, it's impossible not to notice the impact they have on us. Everyone is quieter afterwards and most of us skip lunch in the cafeteria that day. I know we all feel the same after studying the pictures, and still we keep on wanting to be like them.

I remember once when I was 14 years old. It had been a particularly bad season with hand-outs, news clips, and advertisements, all trumpeting out the Reachables' message. The focus for that season had been on lips. Everywhere you went there were images of what they proclaimed were the perfect lips. Smiling was of course not allowed but rather a peculiar type of pouting which, even after many hours of practising in front of the mirror (don't tell anyone), I could never master. Instead, I looked more like a contorted clown.

Day and night my thoughts were consumed with lips, and they were all I talked about. I became obsessed. Eventually, I cracked under the bombardment in my mind and decided that I would never leave the house again. Not until I had the perfect lips. I know it must sound crazy to you, Diary, but I honestly felt I wasn't worthy to walk outside of my door. You must understand that I do not have the perfect lips. Mine are very thin and they don't have the indentation in the middle of the upper lip. They are the very opposite of the images that were being shown us. I felt like a misfit and didn't want to be seen by others. I didn't want to be laughed at or judged for what I'm not. It lasted about a month and I wouldn't even go outside of my bedroom. It wasn't until my aunt threatened to call the Mirror's Agents to come and get me that I finally agreed to go out again. She said it didn't matter what I looked like, that a Shadow Dweller like me shouldn't worry about becoming anything more. Confusing, don't you think?

That's why I loathe these hand-outs and today was worse than ever. All I can think about is how I don't measure up to the images shown. I'm so ugly compared to them. I'm going to bed now and I really hope that tomorrow will be a better day.

Day 18

We had a visit today at school. It was the Agents of the Mirror, the official security regime. They went around to each class, reminding us of the rules and informing us of recent enforcements. They stood lined up in front of us, dressed in black uniforms and their visored helmets on, making it impossible to see their eyes properly. It was an eerie sight. The classroom was filled with tension as they prepared to read. I caught a glance of the others in the room and everyone looked terrified, even Gale. We all held our breath as one of the officials read in a cold, authoritative voice:

By order of the Mirror,

1. There is to be no talking about the past
2. The reading of Reachable hand-outs will now be mandatory twice a week
3. There is to be no trying out for the Reachables unless all standards are met
4. Absolutely no speaking out against the Mirror (publicly or at home)
5. It is illegal to possess or study history books

They are really tightening up the rules. You should have seen the look on my face when they read out the last one. I was so sure that there was a neon sign on my forehead flashing, *I have a history book hidden under my bed, come and get me!* No one approached me or said anything to me, but I could feel my cheeks redden with a mixture of fear and guilt. Why had Mr Sann given me that book in the first place? Was he trying to get me into trouble? Surely, he must have known about the

Mirror's attitude towards studying the past? I planned to go home straight away and destroy the thing, but I never got to it. I don't know why I didn't. Perhaps it's my anger at the way they treat us or the fact that I struggle to think clearly. I didn't eat that extra apple, just in case I put on extra weight.

I'll have to talk to Mr Sann tomorrow, in secret. I hope he will listen and explain what is going on. I feel so alone right now. I wonder if I can talk to Allister? At least I feel safe around him and I have a feeling that he's a really good listener.

Day 19

I am not functioning properly. My thoughts are scattered and I nearly fell asleep at school today. Sandy had to kick me in English class to wake me up. Just in time too, before Mrs Tretom looked over at me. She has zero tolerance for sleeping in her class, (probably because it happens so often). Her monotonous voice rocks you to sleep like a lullaby. My mind was so groggy and confused that I almost forgot to talk to Mr Sann. Fortunately, a quick smile from Allister, as I passed him in the corridor, brought me back to my senses again.

The strangest thing is that it was as if Mr Sann was waiting for me. When I walked into his classroom, he quietly shut the door behind him and invited me to sit down. Then, before I even had a chance to say anything he spoke,

'Abisha, your time has come. You must study hard and look for the message. Only you are able to find it and you *must* find it. There is so much, so many people depending on it. Go home now and study the book. Be very careful not to tell anyone about it. You will be protected as you open it, Gentle has made sure of that. Don't be afraid. I know that much rests on your shoulders, child, but you were born to carry it.'

That was it, and with those cryptic words he told me it was time to go. I tried to protest, saying that I had questions that I really needed to ask him. But he stopped me mid-sentence,

'Abisha, it is not safe to talk anymore. You must leave. We are being monitored and they will be here any minute. Please trust me. I cannot tell you more, except that I knew your father and I am here to help and not to harm you.'

I was about to beg him to explain more when I was interrupted by a knock on the door. Two Agents of the Mirror stormed in. They came up to us and shouted aggressively,

'What is going on here? What are you talking about?'

I was terrified and couldn't speak. Fortunately, Mr Sann took over, as if he had been prepared for this.

'I asked to talk to Miss Abisha. She has not been doing her homework properly and I have reprimanded her and gone through some rules and guidelines with her. We were just finished and she's leaving.' He turned towards me and said sternly, 'You are to go home directly, child. Remember what we have spoken about and don't forget to do exactly what I have told you.'

He motioned for me to leave and, before the Agents could ask any more questions, I picked up my school bag and left. I turned around at the door to look back at Mr Sann one more time and I saw his left eye close, giving me a friendly wink before he continued talking to the two Agents in his room.

I hardly know what to do with the whole experience. I feel conflicted and left with more questions than answers. Who is depending on me? What is this message I'm supposed to uncover and who is this 'Gentle' that Mr Sann mentioned? And, most of all, how did he know my father?

The book is in front of me, next to you, Diary. I recovered it from underneath my bed, but I haven't opened it again. Do you think I should? Do I dare?

What if the Mirror finds out about it. Will they send the Creatures on me?

I'm just a fat girl who wants to be thin and now I seem to be caught up in something that is way over my head. What am I going to do?

Day 20

They really frightened me today. I hardly dare to tell you what happened in case they find out I'm writing this. They came to me again, the Creatures. I was out doing some errands for my aunt when I suddenly felt their chilling breath down my back.

This time they weren't very careful. They didn't seem to care that there were others around, although no one noticed the Creatures except me. I felt their grasp on my skin, it pulled and hurt.

'Don't think that you're anything, girlie, don't believe that you can change anything. Failure is your inheritance and fear your life's companion,' they hissed at me in unison.

'We will see to it that you suffer and regret that you ever tried. Stay in the shadows and know where you belong.'

Their words are etched into my mind. Agonising, like Mrs Tretom's nails when she scrapes them on the blackboard in order to get out attention. Violent, commanding, awful. I think they're right, you know. I shouldn't dare to dream. How many times has my aunt not told me that my dreams will get me into trouble?

I've hidden the book again, there is no use in me looking in it. I know I can't do anything right now anyway. I don't know what Mr Sann was trying to tell me, I find it difficult to even remember his words. After today's events I don't even want to try. My aunt forced me to eat dinner tonight and the feeling of a full stomach is tormenting me. I need to go and throw up.

Day 21

I admit what I did last night was not one of my smartest ideas. The stench of half-digested food filled the whole bathroom. I lay on the floor, weak and ashamed. Tears ran down my face and my stomach cramped in pain. I lay there for what seemed like hours, staring at the bathroom ceiling, searching for some sort of guidance and meaning. I cried out into the darkness for help but my words just echoed back to me, taunting and comfortless. I must have looked pathetic lying there and I know that I felt it. Something in me cried out believing that someone might see me, hear me and even help me. But after a few hours all that remained was my tears, my emptiness and the stench around me.

Today started in a tidal wave of hopelessness. I lay in bed under a blanket of sadness. My mind was filled with self-absorbed fear and desperation about my situation. I didn't want to get up and planned to stay in my room all day.

A knock at the front door shook me out of my thoughts and as my aunt was out I had to put on my clothes to open it. I was embarrassed when I saw Allister standing there. Sheepishly, he said,

'Hi Abisha, I was just walking by and wondered if you wanted to go to the bakery and sit and talk a while.'

I was totally shocked and happy to see him there. I like Allister – I really like him. He makes me feel good about myself. He is so warm and relaxed and doesn't seem to let the valley affect him. I wanted to go with him and sit and talk and share some of what has been happening to me recently. But I didn't dare, and after last night there is no way that I can be close to any form of food, so the bakery was out of the question. I didn't want to go into details with him so I lied,

'Sorry Allister, I already have plans for today and I really don't like the bakery.' (Not a total lie, I mean, I'm sure I'll think of *something* to do today and I don't like the bakery, at least not since my last time there.)

He looked genuinely disappointed, shrugged his shoulders and suggested maybe another time. Just as he was about to leave he said,

'You need your strength, Abisha, this is not the time to be disappearing. You must take care of yourself and make sure that you give your body what it needs. There are people who care about you.'

I didn't know how to respond. His words evoked strange feelings in me. I'm not used to someone showing love and concern for me. It feels like he cares. I like it but it scares me at the same time. I didn't say anything back or promise anything. He has no idea what I'm dealing with inside or what I went through last night. I wanted to scream at him, *You just don't understand. It's easy for you. You have everything under control. My life is a mess, just leave me alone!*

I didn't dare to say any of this, but I sensed he understood something of my dilemma. He left saying,

'I know it's hard for you right now, Abisha, I understand much more than you think. I just want what's best for you. I'm here to help you.'

I didn't answer him. I simply thanked him and shut the door in his face. Now, as I sit here alone I truly regret I turned him away. I feel so alone and I could really do with his support right now. Without you, Diary, I'm not sure how I would survive.

Day 22

I did it. I took up the book and studied it some more. Talking with Allister yesterday helped clear my mind and decide – what have I got to lose.

There are so many facts in the book. Detailed descriptions about Genville, who did what and when and so on. I haven't found any coded messages yet, but I'll keep on reading. I struggled with headaches and dizziness today and my stomach was full of acid. I didn't have the strength to go outside, even though the sun was shining and the mountains were calling to me. I need to store up my energy so I'll be able to go to school tomorrow.

Afternoon

My aunt is definitely acting strangely. She was extra talkative today and started going on about the Festival. The Festival is an annual event and one of the high points of the year in our town. People come from many different districts and it is one of the few times that you see people smiling around here. The sound of laughter can be heard long into the night. Families and friends spend time together and everyone dresses up in fancy clothing. It is also one of the few days when everyone is free from work. *A special treat* the Mirror usually reminds us, as if doing us a great favour or something.

The Mirror … that reminds me of the only negative part of the day. At 2.30 in the afternoon it makes a public announcement, which is meant to encourage and inform the people. All it really does is leave us with a chilling, troubling sense that something is terribly wrong with us. But apart from that, it is a fun day. I enjoy the masquerade and love to plan what I'm going to be dressed up as. For many years I dressed up as a princess. I loved to imagine that I was born into royalty and that I had a special task and position in the world. Last year I went as a tulip, which was not quite as inspiring, I have to admit.

The extra exciting thing with this day is that it also happens to be my birthday! It's my special day, even if I have to share it with others in the valley. Did I tell you that this year I turn 18! Me, finally an adult (whatever that means). I'm excited and something tells me that this year is going to be important for me. I've longed for this day for years, desperate to be free from my aunt. Perhaps now I can move out and find my own apartment, but then I'll have to find some work. One step at a time. Anyway, back to my aunt. This is what she said to me this morning,

'Abisha, my dear, I've been thinking about this year's Festival and I thought we could go together this time. It'll be fun! Also, don't worry about finding an outfit, I'll sort everything out for you. After all, it's your special day, you turning 18 and all.'

There was something strange in the tone of her voice, like she was trying too hard. Too interested, but for all the wrong reasons. She's never called me 'my dear' before, so that made me suspicious straight away. She has never shown much interest in my birthday either and certainly never offered to help me with my outfit. I've always had to arrange it myself and organise my own celebrations. Something just doesn't add up. I answered her,

'Thank you, but no thank you. As usual, I'll fix my own outfit and I don't need your help at all.'

She looked disappointed and even frustrated, but I didn't care. She can't start changing everything now and it's really too late for her to be interested in my life.

The cool thing is that I've come up with a new idea for my outfit and I don't want anyone else to know about it, not even Sandy. It's from a picture in the history book that Mr Sann gave me and I'm going to design my costume from it. I love to sew. I find it so freeing to be able to create something of my own. I found some old materials in our attic and will try to patch something together from that. I just need to keep it hidden from my aunt now. I still can't shake off the sense that she's trying too hard, trying to cover something up.

I spent a long time in front of my father's photograph tonight, something I haven't done for years. It was soothing and reassuring. I stared into his eyes, searching, searching. Those eyes of his. I know they're alive, I can sense it. I'm sure that they are trying to tell me something, but I just can't work out what. Perhaps I'm going crazy. I seem to be obsessed with secret messages at the moment.

I have some good news though. I was able to do up my belt one notch less today. The dizzy spells are worth it! I will be thin.

Day 23

Today was a dark and gloomy day. I didn't talk to anyone at school and came home early with the excuse of not feeling well. I'm overwhelmed, dear Diary. There is a volcano inside of me and it feels ready to explode at any moment. My body is racked with pain and I know that I need to eat. A battle rages in my mind, I wonder if I'm I worthy of eating? Should I allow myself food? A part of me wants to punish myself for being so stupid. The only way I know how is to not eat. Surely a fat person can't be worthy of love?

As long as I can remember, I've felt fat and ugly and that something is terribly wrong with me. The mirrors on the walls have always followed me and mocked me with their messages. But not only the mirrors, there have been other people as well. Even as a young girl, when I walked through the streets people would stop and stare and say things like,

'You look funny! What happened to you when you were born?' Other children would turn to their mothers and ask, 'Why does she look like that, mommy? What's wrong with that girl?'

My aunt never said anything about my appearance, neither to affirm nor challenge their insinuations. Her silence only served to confirm the voices around me. I learnt to cover myself up when we walked into town, with baggy clothes and hats on my head, anything to disguise myself. I felt like a freak and desperately wanted to become invisible to the world around me. When I was old enough to start reading the Reachables' hand-outs, my fears only solidified.

The hand-outs are horrible, but it is the mirrors I hate the most. Today, it felt as if every mirror I passed was empowered with a sinister energy. Hate emanated from them and made me tremble. My eyes felt forced to look into them and as I did I saw my reflection and winced. An ugly, stupid, revolting and fat girl looked back at me. I hate her and wish she had never been born. And yet she confuses me. How did I turn out like this? My father was clearly a handsome man and my mother, well, I've no memory or photograph of her but she can't have looked that bad.

By the time I reached home I was desperate. I wept and wept and, even though I know it is illegal, I threw my jacket over the mirror in my room. I just couldn't bear another reminder of my awfulness. I don't know how I could have been so stupid as to talk to Allister. How could I've ever thought that a kind and special guy like him could ever be interested in talking to me? My stomach growled with hunger pangs all afternoon, but I didn't care. My body can scream all it wants to but I'm not going to listen to it.

After hours of weeping my hopelessness got the better of me. I wanted it all to end. I walked outside onto my balcony and stood there for a long time. I moved to the edge and looked down. We live on the sixth floor and it is high up. The palms of my hands broke out into sweat – I hate heights. I moved back from the edge and was reconsidering if this was such a good idea when I heard a voice in the air screaming at me,

'Just do it now. Jump! Now!'

It was demanding, aggressive and persuasive. I felt compelled to obey it and moved towards the edge, preparing myself to jump.

Suddenly, a beautiful golden eagle flew past me. Its appearance shook me and images of my father passed through my mind. Somehow I knew that he would have been heartbroken to see me end my life like this. Peace filled my senses and I knew this was a mistake. A gush of wind, which came as the eagle passed by, blew me away from the edge. Before I could change my mind again, I rushed back into my room and slammed my balcony door behind me.

I'm shaking as I write to you, Diary, to think that I nearly ended everything. What's happening to me?

Day 24

I dreamt again last night, one of those wonderful dreams I had as a child. In the dream I was a young girl and there were flowers in my hair, beautiful white daisies. I danced and danced in a field of flowers and as I spun around, suddenly my father's face appeared in the sky. He was calling to me and then I heard him say these words over and over again,

'Hold on a little longer child, courage runs through your veins, hold on a little longer sweet child, remember courage runs through your veins'.

As he spoke, power flowed through me. I no longer felt hopeless but loved and I knew all would be well. It was painful to wake up and realise it had only been a dream. How I long for my father to be here with me, I know he would help me to make sense of the chaos I find myself in.

Anyway, I realise that I must have sounded quite dramatic yesterday. I'm so sorry about all my draggling on about my emotions. It's almost ridiculous now to think that I was caught up in such hopelessness and self-pity. It's all so strange. Did I imagine that aggressive voice? What about the eagle, where did it come from? It makes me shudder to think what would have happened if it hadn't flown by.

I feel much better today, probably because of my dream and that I was able to talk to Allister again. I don't know what it is with him, but he is able to help me sort my head out. I even let down my guard with him a little today and it felt both good and absolutely terrifying! I took a really big risk and told him about the book. I know what you must be thinking, how I could be so dumb, but I feel I can trust him and it just came out. He didn't seem surprised at all. He actually encouraged me to look inside of it and promised not to let anyone know about it.

We went for a long walk together and I was amazed when he took me to my favourite place by the fountain. He seemed, instinctively, to know that I love being there. We sat there for a while in silence, listening to the sound of the water. It was calming and refreshing as always. Allister took out two yoghurts and passed me one. I protested wildly at first and said I wasn't hungry. The angry growling sounds coming from my stomach spoke otherwise and he looked at me with a mixture of seriousness and playfulness and said,

'Just eat it Abisha. It won't hurt you, take a bite.'

I almost gagged on the first spoonful and all of my reflexes wanted to throw it up again. It's frightening how my relationship to food has changed in such a short time. I used to love eating and now it feels like a battleground. Food has become my enemy. I forced myself to take one more spoonful of yoghurt and then I had to put it away.

'I'm sorry, Allister, I just can't eat any more,' was all I could say. He didn't push me and we sat having a relaxed conversation about school, our classes and what we are learning. He seemed to enjoy letting me talk. There is a sincerity about him that disarms me. I realised that I'm used to having my guard up around people. Strangely, when I'm with him, I don't feel that I need it. After a while I dared to bring up what was on my mind.

'Allister,' I asked him cautiously, 'Do you ever dream? Dream that there is more to this life than we know in the valley? Do you ever wonder if perhaps this is not all there is, and that somehow things are hidden from us? I think about this sometimes and even more since you and Mr Sann arrived in the valley. Where do you come from? Why have I never seen you before?'

I had a lot of questions and understood that they were not easy to answer. I looked at him cautiously and saw the tension on his face as he prepared to answer me.

'Abisha, there's much that you do not yet understand and even more that I can't share with you. I wish I could, but we must be careful as we can never be sure whether or not we are being watched. Yes, I dream often and have done so my whole life. I can't tell you yet where I come from. You must trust me and believe that I'm your friend. Things are not as they seem here and much of what you know and have been taught is not real. There are other places and even other people beyond Genville. This is a season of awakening for you and it must be very confusing. It's important that you do not listen to fabrications about yourself.'

I didn't understand what he meant and asked him to explain more. He continued,

'There's a time of great shaking coming soon to this place and we must be very careful. I wish I could tell you more, but I'm not permitted to at this point. Search deeply into the book Mr Sann has given you and you will understand more.'

His reply was cryptic but genuine. I don't understand how or why he has come into my life at this time, but I'm very thankful that he has. I glanced over at him and he looked as if he had something else to say, something important. He leaned over and then cautiously but with great authority said,

'Abisha, you are not fat.'

I was embarrassed and taken back by this comment, how did he know that I had been feeling that? Can he read my mind? I didn't know what to answer. I managed to stumble out a few syllables,

'What, I … I um …'

It was no use, I was exposed. He continued,

'Don't let them get to you, Abisha, protect your heart and cover up your mirrors. Watch your steps over the next few days. Take everything you need with you on the day of the Festival. They know that their time is short and will try everything in their power to stop you.'

I had no idea what he was talking about and was desperately trying to make some sort of sense out of it all. I couldn't ask anymore questions as Allister said,

'Come, it is time for us to go. I've said all I can, perhaps too much. Quickly, we must leave now and get you home safely.'

It was an uncomfortable journey down the mountain after that. I was stunned by our conversation but Allister was unwilling to explain anymore. He kept looking over his shoulder all the way home and I was relieved when we finally made it back to my house.

I looked up the word fabrications in the dictionary – it had two different meanings:

1. *To create or produce something*
2. *To deceive, to tell a lie*

I wonder which one Allister meant?

Day 25

I had a dream again last night, and this time it was a bad one. The Creatures came to me and they were larger and even more terrifying than when I've encountered them in reality. There were about five or six of them grouped together. They circulated above my head so quickly that I could barely make out their grotesque forms as they swirled above me. They mocked me as I lay there, spitting out their distaste for me. I froze with fear as they began to tape my mouth together with a thick, black tape. I tried to cry out, but all that came out were muffled sounds. I tried to rip the tape off, but it was as if it was scorched into my skin. Their accusations echoed repeatedly into the night air and I was left with no choice but to listen.

You cannot do it, you are born for failure. No one will ever listen to you, you are a coward and a wimp and nothing good will ever come of your life.

Each word penetrated my soul and I felt like my lifeblood was being sucked out of me. I was powerless to resist or refute their accusations. When I woke up, I was drenched in sweat, and exhausted.

The effects of the dream lingered long into my waking day. I must have looked terrible because Sandy asked me how I was after history class.

'You're so pale, Abisha. Is everything all right? You look as if you've just seen a horror movie. What is going on with you recently? It feels like you are shutting me out of your life. You haven't talked to me for days and I miss our swimming.'

She had a lot to say but I just didn't feel up to answering her. Sandy has always been a good friend, but

I have no energy for her right now. I passed her off with a simple,

'I'm fine Sandy. I just didn't sleep that well last night. I can't really talk right now. I'm going through some stuff. Just give me some space.'

She looked hurt and not convinced by my reply.

'All right, Abisha. I'll leave you alone for now, but you do worry me and don't think I don't see what you're doing to yourself. You're fading away and don't look well. You really need to eat more. Just think about what's happened to the other girls who've done this to themselves.'

She has no idea what she's talking about, I think I look fatter than ever and certainly not like I'm fading away. People can be so stupid sometimes. What mirror is she looking into? Certainly not mine, mine shows clearly that I'm fat, fatter than ever. I blame her words and the dream for what happened next. I just blew everything.

I was on my way home from school when I passed the bakery. The smell of freshly baked donuts permeated the air and after the terror of last night I found the familiar smell comforting. I decided to go in, just for a few minutes. Not to buy anything, I told myself, but only to look and smell. That was my plan anyway.

I saw Mrs White behind the counter. Mrs White is the owner of the bakery and the person I feel the safest with in the valley. She recognised me and gave me one of her famous smiles. When she smiles her whole face lights up, her blue eyes twinkle and it's as if sunshine fills you. It's contagious and all you can do is smile back. As a child I thought she was the most beautiful woman I had ever seen, even though she looks nothing like the images of beauty that the Mirror feeds us with. She has wrinkles all over her face, which become even more visible when she smiles. She has that warm and cuddly look, like a child's best teddy bear. Soft, round and approachable. She radiates love and purity and when she talks to her customers she manages to make each person feel as if they are the most important person in the room. I've always loved this place, because of the way it makes me feel.

I looked around at the ceiling and walls of the bakery. Everything is beautifully decorated. White ornaments around the windows and walls. I had heard that every shop was decorated like this before the Age of the Mirror. The owners would decorate in ways that reflected their passion and part of the joy of going shopping at that time was to see the beauty and originality reflected in each store. Now, everywhere you go everything is plain and cold. I've often wondered why Mrs White had been allowed to keep her decorations up. Many stories circulate, but I once caught sight of a van-load of bread being shipped to the Reachables' headquarters and I'm convinced that has something to do with it. Her presence invokes respect and I'm sure that even the Reachables are a little afraid of her. Suddenly, I heard her call me over,

'Hello, beautiful Abisha. I haven't seen you around for a while. Where have you been? You haven't been sick, have you? You look very pale and thin. What are you doing to yourself? You look like you are wasting away.'

Odd, that she would use the same words that Sandy had used earlier today. What is wrong with everyone? Can't they see that I'm fat? She looked at me with such tenderness as she spoke, as if she knew me, perhaps even loved me. I really didn't know how to answer her. I couldn't be angry with her and it was much harder to dismiss her than Sandy. For a split second, doubts filled my mind and I questioned why I was dieting in the first place. Perhaps I wasn't as fat, I thought.

She spoke again and I snapped out of my thoughts,

'Here, I have a gift for you, a plate of your special donuts. Let me load them up for you. They're on the house, and send my greetings to your aunt for me.'

Before I knew what was going on or could protest I found myself walking out the bakery with a box of four donuts and a smile on my face. I felt strangely free and alive. When I came home I opened the box and saw that they were the best kind: chocolate covered with vanilla cream in the middle.

The smell was intoxicating and before I could stop myself I started to take my first bite. I'm not proud to tell you what happened next. I ate the first one and realised, as each bite went down my mouth, just how hungry I really was, desperately, ravenously hungry. I had denied myself for so many days that I had forgotten what joy there was in letting my tastebuds come alive again.

It all felt so wonderful at first, but then I found that I could not control myself. Desire and longing led to obsession and I stuffed the second and the third and then the fourth in my mouth. I was overtaken by a frenzied binge and what began as something wonderful ended with a bitter aftertaste. I wasn't even aware of how many I had eaten until after I took the final bite of the last one.

As if awoken from a drunken stupor, I suddenly realised what I had done and a wave of guilt and regret washed over me. I felt so full and so fat. My stomach was bloated and I had to undo my jeans button in order to breathe freely. And then I did it again. I ran to the bathroom, stuck my fingers down my throat and threw the whole lot up.

It was repulsive. I knelt by the side of the toilet seat with the smell of regurgitated donuts bombarding the air and wept. I wept so deeply, that I'm not sure how long I lay there. I cried for my father, that I longed for, I cried for the fear that had been building up inside me. I wept because of all the tension and strange events of the past few weeks and for fear of becoming fatter.

Now that it is over, all I'm left with is a hollow emptiness inside of me again. I feel so weak and ashamed. The Creatures were right. I'm a failure and nothing good will ever come out of my life.

Day 26

I don't want to talk about what happened yesterday. I want to forget about the dream, Mrs White and all those donuts down the toilet. The Festival is in two days and I'm excited. My outfit is ready now and I know no one will recognise me. It's exhilarating to think that I've come up with something all by myself and that no teacher, no adult and no Reachable is involved.

My aunt has been rushing about the house, getting things tidy, and the town is swarming with excitement and preparations. I told my aunt that I don't want to have any type of birthday party and she looked relieved, 'That's a good choice, Abisha. It's really nothing special to celebrate anyway, you turning 18.' Not exactly the most loving comment I've ever heard, but I guess she's probably right. It's just another ordinary day. The strange thing is that, deep in my heart, I don't believe it will be.

There's a lot of activity in the valley today and I saw truckloads of mirrors being sent in. The Reachables were putting them up all afternoon, two or three outside of every shop and house. It doesn't add up. Usually they only send in more mirrors every three years. I haven't seen this many mirrors enter the valley in one go before. I wonder why they are doing this now and just before the Festival too? The atmosphere becomes more oppressive for every mirror they uncover. A dark presence has settled in the valley and it makes me feel uneasy.

Afternoon

I'm in shock, Diary, and I don't know what to do about it. I spent a long time reading in the history book this afternoon and I found something that I don't understand. I was on page seventy-eight and was just about to stop reading, as it was getting a bit boring, when I came across a picture. You won't believe who it was. It was my father! I know it was him, I would recognise those eyes anywhere. His name was different and he was dressed in clothes that I've never seen, but I know it was him. It said that he was working on some sort of special project. Strange. What does it mean?

I kept on reading and I read that in the year that my father died, a reprogramming had taken place throughout the country. All newspapers, files and history books had been rewritten, facts modified. The Mirror had sent a group of people to go through the land and erase all traces of the time before that point. New schools had been established and all teachers were forced to be retrained in a new education programme, issued and overseen by the Mirror. Teachers all over the country were taken in for questioning, some of them were imprisoned. A few were allowed out if they made a vow to abide by the new regulations. All new teachers were educated by the Mirror, dictating what curriculum they were to teach as well as their teaching techniques.

Was this the message Mr Sann wanted me to find? Was he one of the teachers from the old regime? Was that what made him seem so different? What about Allister? How does he fit into all of this? Who was my father anyway? I can't make sense of everything and feel like I'm going crazy!

Day 27

I keep thinking about what I read yesterday. I don't know what to think and who to trust.

When I arrived at school today there was an uneasiness in the air. There were far more Agents of the Mirror around than usual. I managed to dodge them and went straight to our history class, which we always have first thing on Friday mornings. I noticed that Mr Sann wasn't there. I was disappointed but guessed that he must be ill. Another teacher stood in front of the class. I didn't like the look of him at all, he made me feel frightened. I sat down at my place and he glared at me. Then he spoke,

'Good morning. My name is Mr Ridge and I'm your new history teacher. Mr Sann will not be coming back. He has not measured up to the Mirror's requirements for a teacher. We will be going over all that he has taught you these past few days and we will make any necessary adjustments if any of his teaching has been out of line with our values. None of you should attempt to contact him in any way. Be assured that he has been removed from your lives forever.'

As I listened to Mr Ridge, I felt as if someone had punched me in the stomach and knocked all of the air out of me. I crouched down in my chair, trying to hide myself. Terrifying thoughts shot through my mind. What did he mean, Mr Sann was gone, replaced? What was I to do now? Did they know about my connection with him? I needed to find him and talk to him. Now, more than ever I needed to get a hold of him and he was gone.

The history class proceeded but I was trapped in a haze of confusion and shock. Desperate to get out of there, I could hardly wait for the bell to ring. When it finally did, I was about to rush out when Mr Ridge said,

'Class, you are dismissed for the day, but Abisha, could you please remain behind? I wish to talk to you.'

I was terrified, fearful of what he might ask me.

'I have some questions for you and I need you to answer me truthfully. The quicker you answer and the more you tell me, the faster you can get away from here. Did you ever talk to Mr Sann outside of class hours and, more importantly, did he ever give you anything?'

I knew that if I were to tell the truth I would put both myself and Mr Sann in great danger and risk of being arrested. I don't usually find it easy to lie, but I knew in this situation I had no choice.

'No, he's never given me anything,' I lied. 'I stayed back to talk to him once, but that's because Mr Sann wanted to tell me off for not doing my homework properly.' I hoped that he didn't notice the way that my voice shook as I spoke or see my legs wobble under my skirt.

'Are you sure that he never gave you anything? A book?' he asked persistently.

I gathered all my courage, took a deep breath and answered him.

'No, he never gave me anything.'

Mr Ridge looked me straight in the eye for what seemed like an eternity and I felt sure that I would crack under the pressure any second. Eventually, he said,

'Well, Abisha, that is good to hear. But be warned that if you are lying to me, we will find out and you will be punished, severely. Now run along.'

I ran out of the classroom and all I could think of was to talk to Allister. I looked for him everywhere but no one had seen him anywhere. Come to think of it he was not in school today at all. I realised that I had no idea where he lived and had no way of contacting him. It scared me that both he and Mr Sann had disappeared and when I need them the most.

Then, as if that wasn't enough, the thing I had most dreaded happened as I walked home form school today. I saw their eyes again, the Creatures I mean. They appeared as I turned around the corner from the old library and stood in front of me, looking at me with searing black eyes filled with rage. I stood frozen with fear at first, but then I felt something rise up inside of me. I looked them straight back in the eye and I saw rays of light hit them. They winced and turned their gaze away from me. There seemed to be something that emanated from inside of me that scared them and they fled. Fled from me, weak little me. What is it? Who am I? Does this have anything to do with the dream I had, the book I'm reading? Perhaps I'm not as powerless as I think?

I forced myself to eat something tonight, not much though. I think Allister is right, this is not the time to be wasting away, fat or not.

Day 28

Today is the day of the Festival and it's my 18th birthday! Happy birthday to me! Even though it's early in the morning the sun shines brightly. Today is my special day and no one is going to ruin it for me. I can feel the energy in the air, there is expectation, excitement. Something tells me this is going to be quite a day.

I've made all the preparations I can. I'm taking you with me to the Festival. I'll hide you and the history book in my handbag. Allister told me to be prepared for anything and to have everything with me that I need, whatever that means. I really wish that I could find him and talk to him. I hope that I'll see him at the Festival. I wonder if he knows it is my birthday? I think I forgot to mention it.

I'm so excited about my costume. It is truly magnificent. I saw a picture of it on page thirty-four of the book Mr Sann gave me and was instantly fascinated by it. There was a whole army of people dressed in it. When I saw, it I just knew that I had to dress like them. It's time for me to go now, I'll let you know how my day goes.

Evening

Everything is so different here in the Cave. They have given me a candle and a pen to write with. I can hardly take it all in. I'm so tired, but I must let you know what has happened.

I knew that something was up as soon as I walked out of my room this morning, dressed in my costume. I met my aunt in the hallway and she stared at me. A look of horror and disbelief appeared on her face.

'Where did you get that costume from?' she finally managed to stammer.

'I made it myself,' I replied and rushed out the house before she could stop me. I didn't want her to hold me back today. She ran after me shouting,

'Abisha, come back. You can't go out like that!'

I should have figured by the look on people's faces as I walked down the street that something was wrong. People my age treated me like air, as usual, but the adults stood mesmerised. Shock, gasps, hands clasped over mouths, fingers pointed. But like I've told you before, I've grown up with people staring and speaking negatively about my appearance so I didn't really stop to think, not as much as I should have.

I made my way towards the field where the Festival takes place. There were hundreds of people dressed up in magnificent outfits. Music played in the background and everything was magical. For a moment, I forgot about all of the dreariness and sadness that exists in this place. People continued to stare at me and I began to feel nervous so I tried to keep myself hidden as much as possible. I found some trees on the edge of the field and stayed amongst them most of the time, watching and looking out for Allister.

By 1.45 in the afternoon, I hadn't found Allister anywhere. I knew that the Mirror would be giving its speech soon and I would have felt much safer if Allister were with me then. Eventually I gave up looking and, by 2 o'clock, I sat hidden at the back of the crowd, ready to listen to the speech. I wish you could have been there to hear it.

The loudspeaker was turned on and a deep, monotonous voice began to speak from it,

'Welcome, inhabitants of Genville, to our annual event. My generosity has been shown to you yet another year and I am sure you would want to thank me for allowing this event. As usual, I would like to thank the Reachables and my Agents for their contributions to our society: their perfection, their beauty and their service. Without them we would not be able to live in such safety and harmony and I am sure that you would all like to join me in showing our gratitude to them.'

We all had to stand up and applaud them at that point and I shuddered with disgust at how unjust the situation felt. Why should we thank them for monitoring and controlling us? As the applause faded away, the Mirror's voice changed to a more sinister tone as it said,

'Now to matters less pleasing to me, I have had reports of a certain awakening. There are those of you who have disobeyed our rules. My reports tell me that there are infiltrators amongst you, sowing in fabrications *(there was that word again!)*, teaching you things that should not be uttered, not even in private.' The voice became angrier and more aggressive, 'There is even a traitor here amongst you and *she* must be punished.'

Everything went extremely fast after that. Out of nowhere, a group of Reachables surrounded me with shouts of,

'Get her!' and 'She's over here.' People all around me were screaming and chaos broke out. 'You can't touch her, not when she's wearing that armour!' someone called and yet another, 'The Servants of the Court are with her'.

I had to ask Allister what happened next, because at that point everything went black before my eyes. Later, when we had made it safely to this cave, he told me that he had been prepared for such an attack, had followed me and kept hidden nearby. He had let out a cry and a group of people dressed just like me had appeared out of nowhere. They had lifted me up into the air and taken me to the Cave where I am now. They tell me that I'm safe here and that all things will be unfolded.

The People of the Cave are incredibly beautiful and noble. I realise now that they were the people I saw in the history book. The pictures I had seen of them are nothing in comparison to seeing them in reality. They are truly magnificent, dressed in golden cloaks that glow as they walk. They all seem to know who I am and salute me as I walk by. It's embarrassing and I feel incredibly unworthy and ashamed. Little useless, weak and fat me, and here is this army of beautiful warriors showing me such honour. My heart and mind are on overload; so much has happened in such a short space of time. I'm tired and I can't write any more. I'm thankful that I brought you with me. I must try to get some sleep. This was not the birthday that I was expecting.

Day 29

It took a while to work out where I was when I woke this morning, but slowly the events of yesterday are catching up with me. The valley, my school class, my aunt, my home – everything feels so far away. What really happened to me? I was rescued from a terrible fate, that much is certain. I feel oddly at peace in this place, as though among friends.

The People of the Cave prepared the most delicious breakfast for me. The smells were intoxicating. Fruits from every season: pineapple, mangoes, kiwis and even strawberries, placed like a rainbow on a circular golden tray. A bouquet of red and white roses in a vase beside me. I had always loved roses but over the past few years growing them has been illegal in the valley. I reached out to touch and smell them and was overcome by the beauty of it all. The aroma of freshly brewed coffee filled the air. How such delicacies could come out of this hidden cave is beyond me.

I tried to resist. I even tried to explain that I couldn't eat because I was f— but before I could form the word on my lips, I looked at their faces and knew I should not say it. I have a strong sense that using the *f-word* is not allowed here. They seemed to understand my battle, though, and gave me a small portion of fruit to eat. They stood watching over me all the time. There was a fierceness and sternness in their eyes that I could not stand up against. The message was clear and non-negotiable – *eat*. I had no other choice and, I must admit, it felt good to fill my mouth with such wonderful tastes. I felt refreshed and revived and stronger than I have for days.

Allister came by to talk to me and I was taken back by how different he looks here. The boyish look that he had in the valley is gone and he appears much more grown-up and regal in this place. I found myself blushing as he looked at me. I really hope he didn't notice, how embarrassing. Fortunately he spoke first,

'You're safe here now, Abisha. There's much that we need to explain to you. It will take a while for you to understand, but sadly we haven't got long. We were forced to act now, even though you are not quite ready. Please cooperate with us and we will help you. You are among friends here.'

I didn't know how to reply except to thank him for rescuing me and tell him how happy I was to see him again. I have so many questions buzzing around in my head.

I spent the rest of the day resting in my room. I feel exhausted. The drama of the past few weeks has caught up with me here and all I can do is rest on the bed that they've provided me with, and write to you of course. It's hard to explain how I feel when I'm here, Diary. All day, I've been searching for something. Something is missing here and I can't quite work out what it is.

Day 30

I know what it is, what is missing, I mean. It dawned on me this morning when I woke up and noticed that the usual knot in my stomach was gone. It is fear. There is no fear in this place. No looking over your shoulder, no glancing to the left or right and no tensed expressions. Even though it is obvious that the people here are occupied with preparing something of great importance, they are clearly not afraid. And then, of course, there are no mirrors here.

I mentioned it to Allister at breakfast today (yes, I ate again, their looks do not allow arguments). His eyes sparkled as he said,

'You're right, Abisha, fear has no place here. We don't operate in that way. Everyone in the Cave has voluntarily given their lives to the cause. We are not afraid. We know that the Mirror doesn't own us. We are, however, on full alert and you've come to us at a time of great tension. These are crucial times and we must be on our guard. The trumpet sounded and I came to your school in response to that call. The Servants of the Court placed me there in order to protect you and to bring you here. That was my first assignment and I've completed it.'

'But, what about Mr Sann?' I asked him. 'What happened to him?' I had been worried about him since he disappeared.

Allister looked away and deep pain filled his eyes and after a few seconds' silence he responded,

'They've taken him and it is a deep sorrow for us, right now. He took a big risk when he allowed himself to be placed at your school, but he insisted saying that he owed it to your father. We are working on a plan to rescue him, but it will not be easy.'

'My father, what did he owe him? Who has taken him?' Again, his words left me with more questions than answers.

'I can't tell you any more at this time, Abisha, except that a big sacrifice was made on your behalf. You don't yet know your value, or who you truly are, but you will, in due time. Too much information too soon will only overwhelm and crush you. We must allow the veil to slowly be removed from your eyes.'

He didn't tell me much more today. I was instructed to walk around the Cave to allow my eyes to become accustomed to the light and my body to the rhythm here. I'm allowed to wander freely, but there is someone who follows me wherever I go. He walks in step with me, persistent and determined. He keeps about two paces between us. When I stop he stops and when I move he moves. At first I found him quite annoying, I've had far too many things following me recently, but I'm actually starting to like him.

His name is Gentle and he is really tall, he must be nearly 7 feet. He's the one that Mr Sann mentioned to me in the valley once and now, finally, I've had the chance to meet him. Covered with golden armour, the light that emanates from him makes it impossible to look directly at him. He carries a silver sword by his right side which sits perfectly in his belt. I haven't seen him use it yet, but something tells me he's a trained warrior and wouldn't hesitate to use it at the slightest hint of danger. Had I met him in any other situation I would have found him terrifying, but here, in this place, his presence is strangely reassuring. It's his eyes that give him away. They are light green, and whilst they penetrate right through my soul with their intensity, they are full of kindness. His presence soothes me and I'm happy not to be alone.

It is eerie when I walk past them, these Servants of the Court; they are polite and treat me with such respect. They salute me and greet me with things like: 'We are honoured', 'We have waited long for you' and 'We stand as your servants'. It makes me feel terribly uncomfortable. Shouldn't I be the one thanking them? They risked their lives to save me. I just don't understand why they seem so happy to have me here.

Day 31

I discovered something special today. It seems that these caves are located somewhere inside the mountains that I've always been drawn to. No wonder that I've always loved them. The caves are hidden underground and I've no idea how we got in here. I haven't been able to find any kind of opening, not so far anyway.

It is really like another world down here. There are rooms, joining into other rooms and the more I explore the more it seems I have left to discover. What strikes me is the simplicity in this place. Both in the surroundings and in the way that people carry themselves. The walls are cream-coloured and create a sense of purity and peace. Despite their exquisite clothing, the People of the Cave seem totally unaware of themselves and clearly have nothing to prove. They are who they are. There is no jealousy or competition in the air. The greatest difference is the lack of mirrors here. It's such a relief not to be faced with my own reflection all the time.

I explored the caves and there are a number of different rooms. One room must be the kitchen, as this is where they prepare the food. The smell coming from in there is delicious and after so many days of denying myself, it awakens a deep craving inside me. The strange thing is that I get hungry in this place and really want to eat the meals they provide for me. The food here is like nothing I've ever tasted before and my taste buds come to life after what feels like a lifelong hibernation. I was so nervous the first two days about having to eat so often and so much. I begged Allister to not make me eat three meals a day and even tried to hide away some of my food under my seat. Allister caught me out straight away and said,

'Abisha, you must eat. It is absolutely vital that you give your body what it needs. It is crucial that you learn to love and take care of yourself if you're ever going to be able to fulfil your destiny. Feeding yourself is a way for you to do that. I know it has been a long and hard battle for you, but let the food here nourish and heal you. I know you're afraid of becoming … but I promise you that you won't.'

I wanted to argue with him, I wanted to shout and tell him that he didn't understand, that he was stupid, insensitive, controlling, anything to not have to eat so much and so often. But something told me it wouldn't make any difference. I was quiet, I ate and, I hate to admit it, felt so much stronger.

Another room that I found had a group of cosy sofas and cushions on the floor and was some kind of relaxation room. The walls were lined with bookcases, filled with books. I've never seen so many books in one place before and it's amazing to think that they are allowed to read them anytime they want. I saw a group of five reading. Each one sat engrossed in what he or she was reading and oblivious to anyone or anything else around them. As I studied them, I'm sure that the light shining from their armour increased in intensity the longer they read. But I'm probably just making it up. I really hope that I'll be allowed to sit there with them one day.

Deeper into the cave, there was a room which looked like a war council room. A group of warriors were gathered around a large map, talking in soft tones, and it looked as if they were discussing a plan of some sort.

I was shocked to see Allister in there. He looked so wise and handsome as he talked to the others that I found myself gasping for air. Gentle took a step closer to me to see if everything was all right. I must have turned bright red and I'm sure that he had a grin on his face when I answered,

'Nothing is wrong, Gentle, I just, uh, need to get some fresh air. It's very stuffy in here isn't? Let's keep moving.'

We passed a room that had a kind of secrecy about it and it intrigued me. I peeked my head around the corner and only had time to catch a glimpse of a production line which was making some kind of lotion, before the door was closed in front of me. I was curious to learn more, but Gentle motioned firmly with his hand that I was to move on. I really want to know what's going on inside, but despite Gentle having kind eyes, something tells me that you just don't mess with him.

Another discovery I've made, which quite surprised me, is that they have a school down here. I found it just before lunch and I almost missed it. I was getting tired after my morning exploration and was about to return to my room when I heard a wonderful sound, that I thought I recognised from somewhere, from inside one of the doors.

The door was oval in shape and looked different from all the others I had seen so far. I turned towards Gentle half expecting him to forbid me to go in. Instead, his face lit up in a heart-warming smile and he opened the door for me with delight. I saw a class of about forty children and they were all singing. They sat in a circle, not in rows like we do in my school. A teacher stood in the middle of the circle conducting the children as they sang. She didn't have that angry, harsh look that the teachers in the valley have, but rather she had the most amazing smiling eyes. She clearly loved her students. I watched them for a while and I was struck by the energy and fascination in the children's eyes. There wasn't a trace of the boredom and rebellion that the children in the valley have. They looked eager to learn and somehow I felt that their lives depended on it. They are obviously first-class students.

I watched, amazed at the way they studied. Images appeared on a screen in front of them. Pictures of swords, shields and other types of armour flashed before them. After studying the images for a while the children began to sing, creating a new sound for each weapon they saw. This surprised me. Their amazingly sweet and soothing song was connected to weapons of warfare and battle. I realised that this must have been the sound that I heard on the mountain a few days ago. The sound that had brought me such peace. I loved being here in this room, listening to their voices again. I could have stayed there for hours. I didn't want to disturb them today, but I hope that I'll get a chance to talk to them someday soon.

Gentle obviously really liked this room too. His eyes lost that serious, *I'm standing at attention* look, and he seemed to thoroughly enjoy being around the children. I even saw him singing along with them (something that he adamantly denied when I asked him about it at lunch). He's really quite adorable.

We continued walking past the classroom and came across *it*. A door that was unlike the other doors. It was made of solid oak. I was drawn to it, dear Diary, but still … a battle raged inside of me as I came closer to it. It was as if I knew there was great knowledge behind those doors, knowledge that no school has ever taught me or ever could. I placed my hand on the handle, but couldn't bring myself to open it.

Day 32

I've been thinking about my aunt today. I wonder if she is worried about me right now? Will the Creatures come to her? Will the Mirror be watching her? I've thought about Sandy too and I feel so bad about the way I've treated her recently. She's always been a good friend to me and I see how much I've shut her out of my life these past weeks. I really hope that she's all right and that she doesn't get into any trouble with the Mirror because of me.

I asked Allister about them at lunchtime today. (Three meals a day, those are my orders and I dare not resist them, not on this point, even though it is hard to force myself to eat again). He told me not to worry and that Sandy was protected. He wouldn't talk about my aunt and said she wasn't my concern right now. I've worked out by now that he will not answer certain questions, no matter how much I prod him. He did say that my training would start soon, whatever that means.

It's strange being here. No one treats me like I'm an ordinary girl. It's as if they see something in me that I'm blind to.

I have so much to discover in this place. I went past that door again today but still I could not open it.

I'm becoming impatient. I don't understand why I'm here and I want some answers. I wanted to throw up their lunch today, just throw it up and walk out of the Cave. I can't understand all they tell me. If I'm so special, why do I still struggle with such doubt about who I am? I want to find out more about my father and what has happened to Mr Sann. I want to help rescuing him from 'them' – whoever they may be. So many thoughts fluttering around in my mind.

Help me, dear Diary!

Day 33

There is an uneasiness in the Cave today. They said the Creatures are on their way, that the Mirror has learnt of my escape. I overheard one soldier report that all through the valley people are looking for me and that the Mirror has my face displayed on all the mirrors across the valley. Such an upheaval over me, it's quite beyond me. I mean, has all of this trouble come on me just because I tried out for the Reachables?

Just as well that my training began today.

First, they took me to the Armoury Room, where they keep all their weapons. I was told that I could choose a shield, a helmet and a sword. Allister was very clear,

'It's important that you choose your weapons yourself. You must know them and keep them with you at all times. They must become a part of you, your greatest ally.'

I had never seen a place like this before. All around the room there were row upon row of all sorts of weapons. They were organised according to colour – gold, silver and bronze – swords, helmets and shields of every shape and size. It was quite overwhelming, just being in the room.

I tried a few swords, but was stunned by their weight. My arms were not strong enough to hold them, not even for a minute, let alone lift them up and fight with them. (I wish that I had not skipped so many PE classes now). I was embarrassed by my weakness and lack of knowledge and really hoped that Allister and Gentle hadn't seen me drop the sword.

I was about to give up, feeling quite ridiculous, when I found a sword I liked. It had a simple gold crested handle with a little image of an eagle on it. It looked simpler than some of the others but I felt curiously drawn to it and although I was still uncomfortable holding a sword it fitted perfectly into the palm of my hand as I gripped it. The tip was sharp and I could never imagine myself using it on anyone.

The shield I chose also had an image of a golden eagle on it, although much larger and more prominent than the one on the sword. The eyes of the eagle followed me as I turned the shield from side to side, as if it was alive. It was large and covered my whole body, down to my knees. It felt good to hold it up and I felt protected behind it.

The helmet was the hardest to choose. I didn't like the way any of them felt as I put them on my head. They were heavy, uncomfortable and restrictive. I tried to bargain my way out of having to have one at all but Allister stopped me, stating calmly but firmly, 'You will adjust to it quickly, Abisha, and in the heat of the battle you will be thankful for its protection.' I don't really have much to say in this area, I'm not exactly the warrior expert, am I? Finally, I found a helmet that seemed lighter than the others and which sat discretely on my head.

They told me that I had made wise choices and seemed particularly pleased and even amused by my selection of shield and sword.

'Interesting that she would choose *his* weapons,' I overheard them say. 'He would be so proud of her.'

I'm getting quite tired of the feeling that everyone around me seems to know things that I don't.

We were about to walk out of the room when something caught my eye in the corner of the room. It was a piece of white fabric, sticking out form a box of old shields. I walked over to it and as I picked up the fabric I saw it was actually a beautiful banner. It was white, had an eagle in the middle and the word *Verum* written above it. I picked the banner up and asked if I could take it with me. They simply smiled and said, 'It's been waiting for you too. It is your banner and the final part of your armour.'

With all of my equipment ready it was time for my training to begin. How do I even begin to explain what it was like? Intense, uncomfortable and exhausting. The only relief was that Gentle was there with me. It seems that he's not only here to protect me but also to train me. I felt pitiful, swinging my sword back and forth, whenever I could get it over my head that is. Left movements, right movements. We practised for hours and right now I can hardly move my arms, they ache so much.

I felt like such a failure and so ashamed, especially when Allister came to check on me. I wanted to show him that I could fight but all I felt like was crying. He must have noticed because he turned to me and said kindly,

'Abisha, even the greatest warrior must start somewhere. Greatness doesn't come overnight, but takes a great deal of discipline and effort. Today is the first day of a journey for you. The People of the Cave believe in you. I believe in you.'

I turned away from him as he spoke, feeling both encouraged and overwhelmed. What is it that he sees in me that I can't see myself? Tomorrow, they say, I must train with the shield as well. I have to pinch my-self just to make sure that I'm not dreaming. All this is so far away from my old life in Genville. I wonder what Sandy would think of me if she could see me now?

Day 34

When I woke up this morning it dawned on me that if today's training is to be anything like yesterday's, I would need all the strength I could get. I knew that I needed to eat my breakfast, but at the same time I was torn by the shame and fear of becoming, well, you know… A battle raged inside of me and I wished that they could train me for *this* battle which seems far more intense and harder to overcome.

I was just about to give up completely when Gentle came and sat down beside me. He took a plate of different foods, eggs, toast, fruit, coffee and juice and looked over at me. No words passed from his lips but I felt his message – *follow my example child*. There was no condemnation in his look, just compassion and understanding. I was touched. I felt that he sees me and understands my struggle. I began to cry and as I did, Gentle took a napkin and handed it to me discretely. He stretched out his hand and as I took it he led me to the breakfast table, helping me to serve myself. It felt amazing not to be alone.

We ate our breakfast without talking and with every bite strength and hope filled me. Afterwards we trained for hours. Side lunges, reactions back and forth, lifting up my shield. Duck, move to the left. On and on, until all I could see were shields and swords.

After lunch they took me to a room I haven't seen before. Inside it there were rows and rows of mirrors. Before I could even ask about it, Allister spoke,

'We have brought you here to help you learn how to discern and decipher the messages that are sent out of the mirrors in the valley. These are copies of the type of mirrors that are found all over the valley. Here, you will learn to identify and expose them.'

I wasn't that thrilled about having to be in a room full of mirrors. It's been such a relief to be without them these past few days. I walked over to the first one and felt the usual wave of self-hate and criticism wash over me. Suddenly I was so angry about having eaten breakfast and lunch today and felt a strong urge to find a bathroom to throw it all up again. I was about to run out of the room when Gentle spoke,

'Use you shield, Abisha.'

I took it up and held it between myself and the mirror. I didn't know what to expect and closed my eyes, afraid of what might happen. Instantly, the messages coming from the mirror were silenced.

I was shocked at how quickly it happened. Without thinking I lowered my shield and, simultaneously, the negative force from the mirror returned. I pulled up my shield again and the voices disappeared. I looked over at Gentle and he motioned me to continue walking. I walked over to the next mirror and the same thing happened. I continued like this for some time and slowly my boldness increased. I began to relax and trust in the power of my shield. It was a wonderful sensation to have a weapon to defend myself with. How I wished I had owned one before. I thought of the people in the valley and longed to be able to give each of them a shield.

Once I had gone round the whole room. Gentle turned to me and said,

'It is time for you to learn to use both your shield and sword. You have learnt how to defend yourself, now it is time to learn how to attack and destroy.'

His words scared me. Gentle seemed to understand and with great compassion he looked over at me and reassured me,

'There is nothing to be afraid of. Just hold on to the sword and let it do what it is designed for. Hold it up firmly in front of the mirror and then strike with full force. You can do it Abisha, I know what you are made of.'

I took up both my sword and shield and walked over to the first mirror again. As the messages emanated from it, I held out my shield and then Gentle commanded,

'Take up your sword and lunge it right in the centre of the mirror.'

With all the force I could muster up, I plunged the sword right into the heart of the mirror. Nothing happened at first so I lunged at it again and again until, exhausted, I took a step back to see what would happen.

Suddenly, a shrieking sound pierced the entire room and the mirror began to crack into hundreds of small pieces. The glass bits fell and formed a large pile on the floor. Gentle signalled to me to place my sword there one final time and as I did the glass pieces evaporated, leaving only a small pile of ashes behind. Stunned and excited, I looked over at Gentle and he smiled back at me. Hardly above a whisper, he spoke,

'You see, Abisha, I knew you could. You were born for this.'

And so it continued all afternoon. I used my sword on each mirror until all that was left were piles of ash scattered around the room.

Day 35

Today was much like yesterday. Hour after hour of training with my sword and shield. Gentle is in charge of my training and oversees all that I do. Allister comes to check in on me every so often and I feel nervous when he watches. I don't want to embarrass myself or let him down. Gentle is incredibly encouraging to me. He instinctively seems to understand my inner struggles both with eating and learning to fight. His uplifting words strengthen me and inspire me to keep going when I'm tempted to give up. The compassion he shows me makes me feel like a baby wrapped up in blankets, protected and nurtured.

I spent a long time in the room filled with mirrors (all of the mirrors destroyed from yesterday had been replaced in order for me to practise again). I noticed my banner leaning against the wall and realised that I had forgotten about it. I was curious about what I would need it for and asked Allister. He smiled and answered with a trace of amusement in his voice,

'I've been waiting for you to bring that up. Your banner surpasses all of your other weapons and if you should, at any point, lose your weapons or be unable to use them, pick up the banner, wave it in front of the mirror and you will see what happens. Remember, it is your secret weapon.'

He didn't want me to try today, but told me that I should always have it with me when I go out into the battlefield. Battlefield? The closest I've ever come to a battlefield is the netball classes in PE when it felt like the other team was going to crush me and my team. I really wish I understood more about why I'm here and what it is that they see in me. Anyway, I've made a mental note about the banner. Of all the weapons I have, the banner is without a doubt my favourite. I still have no idea why I have to go through all this training, but they are determined that I undergo it and have promised to explain more to me later today.

Afternoon

Finally, the pieces are falling into place. They explained so much to me today. I'm still reeling from the shock of it all and I hardly know where to begin.
Let me start with repeating the conversation I just had with Allister.

We had finished eating dinner together and had a cup of tea together in the relaxation room. We were chatting about nothing in particular when a frown suddenly appeared on Allister's brow and in a serious tone he said,

'It is time for you to understand, Abisha. Your father was a great leader, our leader. He built this place inside the Cave as a haven of training and protection. As Servants of the Court we were trained to be warriors of light. Trained in unmasking the ways of the Mirror, in order that we might defeat it. To be protectors of the city and keep the people safe from the onslaught of the enemy's forces. Your father was very loved and his passion for teaching and training is etched into every pore of the walls here, as well as in the hearts of the soldiers who trained under him.

Your father was working on a heart lotion that could be given to the people to protect them from the lies of the Mirror, Reachables and their propaganda. It was for the sake of the lotion that he was finally taken hostage and killed. The spies of the Mirror found out that he was producing the lotion in secret. We warned him to be careful, that his life was in danger, but your father was a man who knew no fear. He was determined to finish making the lotion and nothing we could say would deter him from working on it. No one knows what happened, except that he was working late at night when the accident happened. Accident is what they called it, but we all know better. There was an explosion and some said that your father was to blame.

Mr Sann was your father's right-hand. They worked together as a team and he had sworn his allegiance to protect your father wherever he went. He was usually always by his side, but that night he had allowed your father to persuade him to go home, "I will be working late. Don't fuss. I'll be fine, go home to your family," your father had told him. He was not there when it happened and has never fully recovered. He always felt that he was responsible somehow. That is why he volunteered to give you the history book. He felt he owed you and your father his life, a price that he may very well have paid by now. We still do not know if he's alive or not.'

Allister's voice became shaky as he spoke of Mr Sann and I sensed great anguish inside of him. He really seems to care about Mr Sann. Allister took a deep breath, regained his composure and continued,

'For years we have watched over you, until your 18th birthday; it was then that the Mirror's grip over your life was to be broken. The Mirror knew that this time was coming, which is why Creatures were following you and tried to threaten you. That's also why the onslaught on your mind and emotions was so fierce, causing you to hurt and starve yourself. The Mirror's aim was to get you to kill yourself before we could get to you and before you could discover who you really are.'

Allister looked at me with deep compassion at this point and I knew his concern for me was genuine. He carried on,

'The Mirror came very close to achieving its goal and when we saw that you were hurting yourself, we were compelled to send in reinforcements. I was one of them. The Servants of the Court have waited, until this time, for you to come and take us into battle against the Mirror and its forces.'

His words shocked me.

'My father, a great leader, killed, murdered and me a leader?' I asked him to explain further.

'Only a child of his can lead the army again and that is why we have waited for you.' (Explains why they've treated me with such respect and awe.) 'You may not feel ready, and in many ways you are not prepared, but because your father's blood runs in your veins, you have the authority and power to lead us. But first you will undergo a great testing …'

That was all he said, and before I could ask him any more questions he left the room and Gentle came to fetch me to take me back to my bedroom.

Day 36

It was a strange day. I still can't believe what they allowed me to go through. It all started over breakfast when I overheard Gentle and Allister talking. Gentle asked,

'Does she really have to do this today?'

Allister replied,

'I know it will be hard for her but the time is very short, we must prepare her as much as we can. We know that they may come for her at any time. The Eternal Law cannot be changed and we can do nothing but wait and let her face her destiny and choose.'

I felt quite unsettled by their discussion and wondered what they meant. Where were they going to take me, what was it that lay ahead of me, and who was coming to get me? Looking back, I'm very happy that I didn't know what was going to happen, or I would have run away immediately.

After we ate, Allister came up to me and said,

'Abisha, today we are going to take you to a room you've not been in before. There you will meet some of your greatest fears. But do not be afraid. You will look into the face of what you dread and learn to overcome.'

I didn't know what to think.

I was thankful for Gentle's guarding presence behind me as Allister led the way. When we came to the door that I was to go into, I discerned a dark presence inside. I couldn't understand why they would bring me to such a dreadful room, here of all places, where they say I'm safe. I know I told you that there's no fear in the atmosphere in the Cave, but at that very moment, it was all I felt.

I looked around the room and saw hundreds of Creatures that belong to the Mirror. I was terrified and I wanted to run – anywhere – just to get out of there. Allister must have sensed how I felt because he quickly placed his hand on my shoulders and looked at me sympathetically,

'We will be here with you all the time. What you see in this room are only images, they are not real and cannot hurt you. But one day you will have to face them in person. You must know your enemy if you are to defeat him in the heat of the battle. What you know, you need not fear. What you've learnt to conquer can no longer control you.'

They took me past images of the most frightening and monstrous beings. Worse than anything my nightmares had ever shown me and more terrible than what I had seen in the valley. There were reptile-like beings covered in scales. The snakes were the worst. Their tongues moved in and out and I felt sickened to my core when I saw them. I've always been afraid of snakes and imagined at times that there was a nest of them under my bed. Some Creatures had the shape of birds, with long talons and beaks that were razor-sharp. Each creature was grotesque, having the form an animal, yet distorted and disfigured in every way.

As I looked at these beings, flashbacks of childhood nightmares came washing over me. My body went cold and into shock as memory after memory of those dreadful nights came flooding back to me. The very images that had tormented me as a child now stood before me. How could I've forgotten? My instinct was to close my eyes and not look as the waves of terror and panic consumed me. I felt like a child standing in front of these images, unprotected and exposed. I wanted to run and hide but Allister wouldn't let me. Kindly, but firmly, he said,

'You must look, Abisha, look them straight in the eye. Observe and know them – once you've seen them for who they really are, they will no longer have any power over you. You're no longer a helpless child, you are your father's daughter. You have the power within you to overcome.'

I turned my face to look at the Creatures and every time I felt too overwhelmed and tried to look away, Gentle held my face and moved it back to look. It all seemed so cruel and I felt confused. Why were they reminding me of childhood terrors now? I thought that they would train me to use my sword, or at least to use my shield to protect myself from the images? I wondered if it was here that I could use my banner. I would even have been willing to use that dreadful helmet at that stage, but all they seemed concerned with was me studying these images.

After what seemed like hours (but what they later told me was only half an hour), I noticed how my feelings towards the Creatures began to change. As I thought of my childhood nightmares, I no longer saw the Creatures but rather the face of my father. I saw how he used to sit beside my bed at night and read me bedtime stories. The stories were always full of adventure and contained a young girl who had to overcome great danger and trials and eventually became the heroine of the story. We would laugh together and then he would hug me and kiss me goodnight, repeating these words,

'Abisha you're my beloved daughter. I'm so proud of you. You're made for greatness but most of all you're created to be loved. Remember that your father loves you. Sweet dreams now.'

I had forgotten these memories but strangely enough now, in front of these Creatures, they came rushing back to me. Fear was replaced with the knowledge that I'm loved, and terror with a kind of curiosity. The Creatures started to appear increasingly helpless and pathetic to me. In the last few minutes of my time in the room, I even thought I saw a glimpse of a young girl captured inside one of the Creatures. I had no idea who these Creatures were, all I knew was that they no longer had a grip on me. I felt exhausted and was ready to get out of there just to see something different. I was relieved when Allister said we could go to the children's room and listen to them.

As soon as we came into the children's classroom the sound of their voices soothed me. The energy and innocence in their eyes was healing after having been in the room filled with Creatures. As the sound of their song washed over me, I felt instantly refreshed and revived. I looked over at Allister and he too seemed caught up in their song. His shoulders relaxed as if a great weight was lifted from them and the tension around his eyes and mouth disappeared. He looked young and alive.

Allister must have felt me staring at him because he looked over at me and our eyes locked. His face lit up in a large smile. I smiled back and then, quickly, looked away. The feelings that he awaken in me scare me, more than any of the Creatures I've just seen. I can't seem to understand or decide over these feelings and I hope that he doesn't notice.

The children's song pulled me away from my thoughts again,

> *We are born to be free, we are born for destiny*
> *Never back down in the face of adversity.*
> *Breakthrough is waiting*
> *Around the corner of struggle and pain*
> *Don't give up, victory is on the way.*
> *We are born to be free, we are born for destiny.*

Allister walked me back to my room after that and we said nothing on the way there. I wanted to reach out to him, to let him know that I was thankful for all that he had done for me. To let him know that I cared and that I wanted to get to know him better. But no words would come out. I could have blamed it on what I had seen in that terrible room, but something tells me that it runs deeper than that. All I could say when he turned to say goodnight was,

'I hope you sleep well.'

He turned to look at me and simply answered,

'Thank you Abisha. I hope you do, too. You did well today. Make sure you get your rest now and prepare yourself. None of us knows what lies ahead, but whatever you may face tomorrow, remember that you're loved by all of us. We have shown you what we can and now we must wait. You have a long journey ahead and your destiny and the destiny of the valley is about to be tested. Remember to choose wisely, whatever you may face.'

His words were mysterious, as if he was hiding something from me. I wish I understood more of what's going on. It scares me to think about the feelings that are surfacing in my heart towards Allister. I like him and I think he likes me too. I'm finding it harder and harder to act normal around him. His presence evokes deep feelings and I wonder what I should do with them. This is so new to me – I've never felt like this before. I wonder if I dare to talk with Gentle about it? Perhaps he can help me.

Day 37

I've been taken again! I don't know where I am or what has happened but I've been taken. It is terrible. That I hid you and a torchlight in my coat is my only comfort right now. I've tried screaming for help but no one comes and the echo of my shaky 'help' taunts me and remains unanswered.

I don't understand. This was not supposed to happen, not after all the training I just went through with Allister and Gentle. Where are they? Why didn't they protect me? Why did they allow this to happen? My mind is confused. Was it all just a dream?

All they've given me so far is water and my stomach churns with a mixture of hunger and panic. I tried to stand up earlier but found the walls around me swirling as if on a merry-go-round. Spinning, spinning, everything blackened before my eyes and then I fell again. That was hours ago and I find myself edging in and out of consciousness.

I don't have the strength to write to you about what has happened these past few hours. You will have to wait, Diary, I am tired, so very tired …

Day 38

It is real. I'm still here in this dark, musty room and there is no escape. The smell is suffocating, damp fumes consume me. The dripping sound has kept me from sleeping. Every time I doze off a persistent *drip, drip* wakes me up. The darkness is agonising. I awoke to black nothingness, searing into my heart and growing into an intense fear. The torchlight is all that keeps me from insanity.

I have little strength right now, after all my weeping and screaming. I know it was not the most sensible thing to do, but I couldn't help it. All the emotions and turmoil of the past weeks have caught up with me and the utter horror of being captured is breaking me. The training I was given training is useless to me now. I don't have my shield or sword with me. A destructive pull inside of me that takes me into the darkness and shuts off my ability to think.

I guess I must try to explain what has happened to me now, even though I hardly know where to start.

After my day in the room with the Creatures, I was worn out and so many thoughts rushed through my mind. I felt partly empowered after my time there, and encouraged that the images were no longer a source of terror for me. It was also wonderful to be reminded of my father's bedtime ritual. That night my father appeared to me in a dream again. His eyes shone and, in that moment, I was overcome with the sense that he truly loved and accepted me for who I was. His kind face was beaming at me as he spoke,

'Be strong, daughter, be of great courage. Nothing can stop you, but you will need resolve. There are still things that you don't understand and there will come a time of testing. Hold on and don't despair. I will be with you, even when everything around you speaks abandonment. Follow your heart and don't doubt your true self. A choice only you can make lies ahead of you.'

His words land flat now in this dark and terrible place. Could he have known what would happen to me? Perhaps it was a warning to prepare me?

I was still dreaming when, suddenly, piercing screams filled the air and woke me. Startled, I opened my eyes and saw two Creatures in my room. I sat upright in my bed, horrified. Although I felt no fear at seeing them after yesterday's practise, I found them revolting to look at: slit black eyes, seething with hate and mocking me with their superiority. Their wings were black, not lustrous and majestic like those of the eagle, but hagged and broken. Razor-sharp edges that looked like daggers. They had the form of a bird yet the head of a dragon, breathing threats at me with smoke and fire. Their voices were like the sound of screeching brakes when a car is about to collide into a wall. A terrifying, high pitch that penetrated the walls of the Cave. Instinctively, I put my hands over my ears, but nothing would stop it. I tried to grasp why they were in my room when, viciously, they screamed,

'We have come to get you, Daughter of the Kind. You're ours and belong to us now.'

I tried to scream for help but before the sound left my lips, they tied a scarf around my mouth,

'No, you won't, little girl. Don't think that anyone can hear you now. There's nothing you can do, nowhere you can go … the Eternal Law protects us and allows us to take you as our rightful prisoner. There's nothing you can do to save yourself – you're ours.'

In desperation I tried to protest, but my cries were stifled by the scarf around my mouth. I looked frantically around for Allister and Gentle, hoping and expecting them to rush into my room. But I was alone and they never came.

The bird-like Creatures approached me. Grabbing hold of me with their sharp talons, they lifted me up and flew me right through the walls of my room. The laws of physics did not seem to apply to them. It hurt to be caught between their talons. I tried to break free but was trapped, and it only hurt more when I tried to move. I felt helpless as we flew past the training room, the armour room and the corridors, towards a door I had never seen before. I looked back into the Cave, desperately searching for someone to help me when, suddenly, I saw Allister. Hope rose in me and I was certain that he would rescue me. But, he just stood there, paralysed, as if some invisible rope held him in place. The sense of betrayal I felt at that moment was more that I could bare. Momentarily, he looked up at me and his eyes were full of pain and defeat. He let out a terrible sigh of resignation and muttered,

'I'm sorry, Abisha. I can't help you. They have a legal right. We are bound. Remember what we have taught you this far.'

His words made no sense and left me devastated. Why? How could he not help me after all that we have gone through together? And then I was taken, flown out of the Cave into the darkness to a place I neither knew, nor cared to know.

Day 39

I don't know how long I've been sleeping. The dripping sound woke me again and it was a relief from the dream I had. It was filled with mirrors and their message was, *Hi fatty, you are ugly, you are such failure. You will never amount to anything. Better to give up and accept the truth. We own you.*

The mirrors seem to have more power in this place and I don't know how to resist them. The ironic thing is that I'm desperately hungry. What I wouldn't give for some food right now. To think that just a few weeks ago I had willingly put myself through this starvation. No one has come or brought me anything, except for the little water that was in the room when I first arrived.

I must try to finish my story, or at least to bring you up-to-date. As I told you, we flew past Allister and he did nothing to rescue me. I'm still angry and in shock that he didn't help me. I thought he was supposed to support and protect me just like he did on the day of the Festival? I wish that I had not seen him at all, because now the image of him standing there passively crushes me. I don't understand where Gentle was in the midst of all this either. He's been my guardian during my time in the Cave, but then when I really needed protecting he wasn't around.

Anyway, whilst Allister looked on, the bird-like Creatures flew me out of the Cave and ascended into the darkness. We flew through the night air and I was petrified as I looked down, caught in the claws of the birds and completely at their mercy. I expected them to drop me at any moment. My body stiffened as I prepared myself to fall. I've always hated heights and it was torturous to be suspended in the air. Sweat dripped from my hands and my forehead and I felt dizzy and nauseous. Still, they kept flying, determined and persistent in their path.

Finally, we arrived at a tunnel. As we entered, cold air hit me and I registered that the tunnel was made of ice. I shivered and longed for my winter coat and gloves. We travelled through it for a few minutes and then a new tunnel appeared before us – this time made of fire. I felt a momentary relief from the cold as the flames warmed my freezing body but, within seconds, they became suffocatingly hot. Flames rose up around us and even the Creatures seemed hesitant to fly through them. They didn't waver for long as instantly they took off again, flying right into the heart of the fire.

We flew deeper and deeper into an underground world and as the heat raged around me I was sure this was the end. I let out a final scream for help and then everything went black before my eyes. I must have fainted because the next thing I remember is being dropped onto this hard floor. I opened my eyes and was astonished to see that I neither had burns on my body, nor did I even smell of smoke. I've no idea how I made it through that tunnel of fire unscathed.

The two Creatures untied the scarf around my mouth and spoke,

'You are ours now, we claim you again. The Queen will visit you at the appointed time. Until then, it would be wise of you to think through your options. She has much to offer you in this place and soon you will need to choose. Until then – enjoy your prison!'

There was no denying the mockery in their voices and they seemed to take great pleasure in my distress.

Once again, I was left with the nagging feeling that those around me know much more about me than I do. And then they deserted me and I was alone in this room.

Afternoon

They came to me again this afternoon. They opened the heavy iron door and brought me water and some form of food. I hardly dared to touch it, as the stench coming from it made me retch, but I was desperate, starving and dehydrated. They spoke again and said,

'Soon you will meet the Queen, and be sure to finish your food, everything is monitored here.'

This Queen, who is she? Something inside of me longs to meet her, but at the same time I feel uneasy in my stomach at the thought of it. I don't feel well, I can't think clearly. I'll write more tomorrow.

Day 40

A peculiar scent fills the air in this place and it is intoxicating and alluring. The longer that I'm here, the more I feel like I'm losing my mind. My thoughts are scattered and fleeting.

I find it harder and harder to remember my time in the Cave. Did I make it all up? I can't seem to recollect what they said to me there. I see a remote image of a sword and a banner, but I can't quite remember what they were for, something about being a warrior, about overcoming something. Not that I care anyway, it has nothing to do with me I'm sure. Here I am, cowering in the corner of this ghastly room like a scared animal. I could never have anything to do with warriors and bravery.

Sadly, I still remember Gentle and Allister, at least vaguely. I thought that they were my friends, that they were there to help me and even that they cared. Remembering Allister hurts most of all, and to think that I was starting to have feelings for him. Now all I feel is anger and hurt.

I realised today that the People of the Cave must be the traitors, that they are the ones who want to harm me. Why was I so foolish as to trust them and even open up my heart to them? Why didn't I hold on to the teaching I've had all my life in the valley: *Don't open up, don't be vulnerable and NEVER trust your lives into another's hands.*

They were right, my teachers, they knew that opening yourself up to someone else would only cause you pain. Allister must have been my enemy all along – taking me from the valley where I was safe and under the guidelines of the Mirror. And to think that I believed he was helping me. I've learnt my lesson now, haven't I?

I bet Allister and Gentle are laughing at me right now, discussing how gullible I am and how easily they could lure me into their trap. To think that I even let them persuade me to eat more. They were certainly out to make me fat. It hurts even to write these things down, I must stop.

But wait, there's one distant memory of children. I hear them singing, calling me, believing in me. What is it they are singing, something about destiny and freedom? I can't seem to remember who the children are or where they come from. Probably just something that I've imagined. You, my dear Diary, are the only record I have of my past, a small comfort in this place. Yet, even you I'm beginning to doubt. Why should I share my life with you? Will you just turn your back on me or laugh at me? Even worse, will you betray me and shout from the mountaintops what I'm sharing with you in secret? I don't even want to know what I've written to you before. I don't trust myself, or you. I'm overwhelmed. I must try to rest.

Day 41

Today everything changed. Early this morning they came to move me. Surprisingly, it was not the two Creatures who came to fetch me, but two girls. They must have been about my age and I was caught off guard to see them. What had happened to the sinister beings that had captured me? The girls were incredibly beautiful and instantly I realised that they must belong to the Reachables – what were they doing in this terrible place?

They didn't talk to me but placed a blindfold over my eyes and led me forward. I had no idea where they were taking me and ominous thoughts rushed through my mind. Faster and faster they pulled me, and when I stumbled at one point, they kicked me and pushed me forward. I completely lost my bearings but was aware that we had made a number of turns, both to the left and to the right. After what seemed like ten minutes, we stopped and they led me into another room. They removed my blindfold and I braced myself for what I would find before me.

It took a few seconds for my eyes to adjust to the light, and when they did, I let out a gasp of shock. The contrast between the place they had just taken me from to the room before my eyes was incomprehensible. It was the most exquisite sight – a room fit for royalty. The ceiling and floor were laden with what appeared to be pure gold. The walls sparkled and were covered with a mosaic of precious jewels. Diamonds, pearls, topaz, emeralds and rubies were just a few that I identified at first glance.

The room was equipped with everything that I could have ever dreamt of. To my left stood a dressing table laden with jewellery of every colour, style and size. There were rings, necklaces, bracelets, diadems, hair clips and tiaras. In the middle of the room there was a canopy bed, draped with sheets of silver. A canvas of golden fabric was strung above the bed. It looked regal and inviting. My tired and worn body longed to lay down on it and sleep away the anguish of the past few days. A glass chandelier hovered next to the bed and sparkled like the stars in the sky. I was mesmerised by the light that radiated from this lamp. Next to the dressing table was one of the largest mirrors I've ever seen, reaching from the floor to the ceiling. Energy emanated from it and I felt a compelling urge to look into it. To my right was a mahogany wardrobe and just beyond that, a bathroom.

I turned to the girls beside me, hoping that they would be able to explain something to me. They remained silent but handed me a golden envelope. They motioned for me to read it and then turned on their heels and left. I heard a heavy click as they locked the door from the outside.

I looked at the envelope in my hands and hardly knew what to do. To be in such an exquisite place after all that I had been through these past few weeks was hard to grasp. I felt like a puppet on a string and the puppeteer seemed to pull me in unexpected directions over which I had no control. I put the envelope on the dressing table, not wanting to open it just yet.

I walked over to the cupboard in the right hand corner of the room. Gingerly, I opened it, bracing myself for anything. I gasped and grabbed hold of the door in order to steady myself. In front of my eyes was the most magnificent display of clothes I had ever seen. Ball gowns, summer dresses, tops, jeans, suits, coats and jackets. There were shoes to match every outfit, high heels, pumps and sandals of all kinds and colours. I tried on a pair of shoes and noticed how they fitted me perfectly. Everything seemed to have been designed just for me, the wardrobe with warm reds, turquoise, cream whites and the blazing green I love so much. I walked back to the dressing table and, with shaking knees, sank down on the chair in front of it. The letter glared up at me and, as fear gave way to curiosity, I tore it open. The words were elegantly written with a golden pen. I began to read,

Dear Abisha,

Welcome to my kingdom. A place of the unexpected, where your deepest, secret longings can be fulfilled. This is my kingdom and here my rules apply, and mine alone.

What you see in front of you, in this room, is my offer to you. All this can be yours if … we will get to that tomorrow when we meet. I have carefully picked out the colours and styles that I believe suit you best. Although you have not met me, I have been watching you for many years now and know what you like and long for. Feel free to use and try on anything you find in the room. It is good for you to know what is being offered you and to evaluate your reward thoroughly.

We will meet tomorrow at 9 am sharp. Some of my girls will knock to pick you up at 8.45. Make sure that you are ready and well-dressed. No one is allowed to appear before me without beauty and perfection. You will only speak

when I address you and require an answer. Sleep peacefully in your new room and I hope that we will become strong acquaintances in this place.

Yours truly and faithfully,

The Queen,
The one and only true and rightful Heir to the Throne

The Queen … she must be who the Creatures were talking about. I've never heard of a queen in the valley before. Who is she and what does she want with me? It frightens me to think that she's been watching me. How and when, I wonder? Even though she appears friendly and has given me a beautiful room, I sense an element of threat in her voice. I'm not sure that I want to meet her tomorrow. Something tells me that she's not the kind of queen that you cross. But for now, all I want to do is explore this room and all the treasures inside of it – and I must go and look in that mirror.

Evening

What an amazing few hours I've had, dear Diary. After reading the Queen's letter I was shaken, but looking into the mirror calmed me down. I was captivated by the image that was reflected back at me. I didn't quite recognise myself, but I liked what I saw. Of course I saw all of my imperfections, but for the first time in my life I felt that there was hope to fix me offered in this room. I decided to look around some more and walked into the bathroom.

I spent the rest of the afternoon in there. It was simply amazing! There was a large, oval bath made of ivory, and all sorts of bath salts, body scrubs and oils lined up beside it. At a closer look, I saw that they were divided up into three different themes. *Relax, purify and entice.* I decided to run myself a bath immediately and chose *relax*.

By the sink there was another row of beauty products: make-up, body lotions, cleansing creams. All the items that I had never really been able to afford, but had heard that the Reachables used. Each was suited just to my skin type, dry.

There was another mirror that covered the left side of the bathroom and it also drew me in. After a wonderfully soothing bath, I must have spent hours in front of that mirror pampering myself and experimenting with different kinds of make-up. I went over to my wardrobe and tried on item after item, matching them with the jewellery and shoes provided.

I almost forgot where I was until I was snapped out of my dream world by a knock on the door. Two girls entered, carrying a silver tray with what appeared to be my evening meal. All types of salads, fruit and some grilled chicken, exactly the way I like it. Just like the other girls they did not talk to me. They were pretty and all I've ever hoped I could be like, although, I thought I detected a trace of sorrow in their eyes. The lunch was delicious and I had no feelings of guilt over eating it as each dish was labelled with its calorie content and there wasn't a trace of fat to be found! This is my kind of place.

I think I could spend an eternity here and never grow tired of trying everything on. To think that all this can be mine. Magical! At one point images of Allister and Gentle passed before my eyes and for a fleeting moment I felt a pang of grief at the thought of not seeing them again. But a long look in the tall mirror soon cured me of that as I remembered that they don't really care for me anyway. I vaguely recall that they took me somewhere after the Festival, but I can't for the life of me remember where and, anyway, this place is far more welcoming and inviting than anywhere I've ever been before. I feel happy here and I look forward to meeting this queen tomorrow. Who knows, perhaps we can become good friends.

Day 42

I am overcome by my meeting with the Queen. How can I describe her to you? She is the most magnificent individual I have ever laid my eyes on. A shimmering silver light emanates from her. Her hair is black as the night sky and drops past her shoulders, something that is forbidden for women in the valley. Her body is perfect in all ways. She has an hourglass figure with not an ounce of fat showing. There is something about her that seemed familiar, but I can't quite discern what. Her nose is sharp and pointed, her cheekbones perfectly shaped. There is not a single line or wrinkle on her face, the perfect complexion, making it impossible to determine her age.

She wore an exquisite gown in shimmering light blue and the fabric cascaded like a waterfall down her breathtaking body as it reached all the way to the floor. There were sequins embroidered into the dress, making her glisten like the ocean as she moved across the room. Glorious jewels hung from her dress, sparkling and mesmerising as if possessing a hidden power. How I longed to be like her.

She stood beside a majestic throne. It was made of gold and embedded with diamonds. She held a sceptre covered with precious stones in her hand. I wanted to reach out and touch it, to somehow own it for myself. She epitomised the image of perfection that had haunted me since childhood and now it stood before my eyes.

I must have stared at her for a long time as she suddenly looked over at me and our eyes locked. I was thrown back for a moment as she scrutinised my face. Her gaze evoked conflicting reactions in me. I felt loved and hated, wanted and rejected, beautiful and ugly, all at the same time. The ambiguity of the moment threw me off guard.

The Queen moved over towards her throne and sat down. Then she spoke for the first time. Her honey-sweet voice penetrated the air, and as she spoke I thought of delicacies, cakes and sweets, the forbidden comforts of this world.

'Welcome, Abisha. Finally, we meet, my sweet child. Welcome to my world, the residence of the Reachables. Did you enjoy your new room? Wonderful, isn't it? I hope you found everything to be to your liking?'

Before I had a chance to reply, she continued,

'I have been watching you, little one. You can trust me, child. After all, I am the mother you have always longed for, I am the vision of your secret longings, I am the mother of all Reachables and now you have a chance to become what you never thought you could attain.'

I was lost for words. I was taken in, I knew it, but I wanted to be like her.

'Here time stands still. We do not look back at the past, we remain as we are without ageing,' she uttered as if aware of my thoughts.

She continued,

'Child, I have an offer for you. Be prepared to choose wisely for I will offer it only once. I repeat, this is your only chance.'

I was thrown off by the trace of threat in her words, but curious to know what her offer entailed.

'I know that you tried out for the Reachables only a few weeks ago. A very foolish move on your part, but one that I have chosen to overlook. I also know that you have been in the camp of my sworn enemies. I am sure that they have filled your mind and imagination with many things now. But be sure, dear child, that they were only deceiving you. Think about it. Did they care enough to stop you from leaving when my birds graciously came to save you?'

Again, before I had a chance to reply she continued,

'No, they do not truly care. They only tried to implant myths into your mind, but here, you will discover the real truth about yourself.'

Her words stung but I could not help but agree with her. There was no denying the facts that no one had been willing to help me. Allister had said something about the 'Eternal Law', but what did that mean? Surely they would have been strong enough to help me if they had really wanted to? I barely had time to finish my thoughts when the Queen continued with her proposition,

'Child, I am willing to offer you the chance to become a Reachable. You will have the body, the face and of course the lips that you have always wanted. You will be able to join the parties and the parades and you will even have a special position as a mentor for young, aspiring Reachables. You will live here with me but will be sent on special missions to the valley. You know that you are a great warrior, but not the kind those nonsense talkers have told you. You are mine. Even as a baby I placed my claim on you. Your father, he gave you to me. It would bring him great joy to have you here with me now. We will accomplish great things together and your destiny will be fulfilled. Perfection is the dream of every woman and I offer it to you. And all that you found in your room, the jewellery, the make-up, the clothes and of course the shoes, they will be yours to keep.'

I was overcome. I was being offered all that I had ever longed for. Then she added the last clause,

'There is one requirement, one small thing that I ask of you in order to receive my offer. You must once and for all relinquish your mind to me. Your past, your memories, your dreams, yes, especially your dreams. We do not want them interfering with your special calling now, do we? You must renounce your rights to everything. You must allow yourself to think according to the rules of my kingdom and let your values be my values. And, one final condition, you can never have contact with those people again.'

She could hardly speak at that point and appeared deeply troubled. She didn't say their names but, instinctively, I knew she meant Allister and Gentle. Once she regained her composure she continued,

'You must allow me to erase all memories of them from your mind. It will be as though you never met them.'

A moment of silence followed, before she concluded,

'You have until tomorrow to decide. And remember – this is the only time that I will give you this offer. If you accept, you will automatically be placed by my side, but if you refuse …'

She spluttered out the last words and appeared unable to continue her sentence. Then she vanished and I was left alone with her offer and two of the Reachables led me back to this place and to you, my Diary.

Day 43

It's early in the morning and as I look around this room from my royal bed and up at the chandelier in the ceiling, I know it's not any ordinary day in my life. Today I must choose.

My mind is plagued with confusion, dear Diary. I dreamt fitfully last night, all sorts of images hovering in front of me. At first I saw a faint picture of my father and his mouth was moving as if he was trying to communicate something to me. Then a picture of a shield shot into my mind, an image of the eagle looking back at me, stern and commanding my attention. I couldn't grasp where it came from or what it meant. I saw Allister, pleading with me about something as tears ran down his face. I saw pictures of shoes, dresses and make-up floating in the sky around me. The last image I remember was that of the Queen looking at me with eyes that switched between green and black in an eerie manner. It was a terrible night and I feel exhausted and unsettled.

What should I choose? I'm not used to this feeling of being able to decide something for myself. We have not been trained for this in the valley. There, all decisions were made for us, our job was simply to accept and obey. What of my father? He is dead and he can't help me now. Surely I can help the others in the valley much more by becoming a Reachable myself? I could give them hope. What about Sandy, I'm sure she would be happy if I could guide her into the way of perfection and perhaps even persuade the Queen to give her the same offer. Yes, surely that would be a better way to help those I know in the valley.

But then I remember the People of the Cave, something they said about me being chosen, special. I can't quite distinguish what it was that they told me, the longer I am in this place, the more clouded my mind is. The fragrance in the air becomes stronger for every hour and where I first found it pleasant, it is now quite oppressive and I find it increasingly difficult to breathe and to think clearly.

I don't even know why I'm even struggling with the choice. I mean, isn't this all I've ever wanted, eternal beauty and a chance to belong? To finally become a Reachable. Isn't that the longing that brought me to this place all those days ago when I first dared to try out for the Reachables? She will call for me soon, I know it, but I'm not ready. Two magnetic fields are pulling for supremacy inside of me. It is my choice, I know, yet something tells me my decision will affect so many other than me.

Afternoon

It is done. I stood before her today and now I'm waiting for them to call me again. I hope I have time to write down what happened before they come for me.

They took me to the Queen this morning and as I looked up at her on her throne she appeared taller and more intimidating than the day before. Her crown was placed firmly on her head, as if glued to her hair.

This time, the room was filled with hundreds of girls dressed in evening gowns. Each girl was placed in a different corner of the room, according to the colour of the gown she wore. The groups were then divided up into nuances of that colour, ranging from shades of light to dark. It was a breathtaking sight. Those in green stood to my left, red behind me, yellow close to the throne and so it continued. Without exception, the girls were meticulously styled. Not a straw of hair was out of place, their make-up was immaculately applied and their clothing was magnificent. Dresses, shoes, handbags, necklaces, earrings, bracelets skilfully chosen to harmonise with their outfits.

The girls appeared to be synchronised with the Queen. As she moved each girl moved accordingly, creating movement in the room. She was clearly their leader and the centre of attention and power in the room. Every eye was fixed on her, ready to imitate her next step. The movement in itself was captivating yet, strangely enough, I felt that something was missing. I couldn't decide what it was exactly but I shuddered as a cold draught blew across my back. The Queen began to speak to the girls. She didn't address them by name, but instead by colour. She was clearly irritated as she spoke,

'Reds, stand straighter, you are slacking. Tidy up your dresses, you look scrappy. Yellows, stop slouching, stand tall, chins up, heads straight forward. Greens, who did your make-up this morning? Get it fixed immediately, I can see your skin through it.'

She clapped her hands violently and immediately a group of stewardesses appeared. Each one carried a box overflowing with make-up, mascara, lipstick, foundation, brushes, rouges. With lightning speed they went to each girl dressed in green, fixing up a little eyeliner on one, extra powder on another.

Watching them, I suddenly became acutely aware of my own face. What did I look like? My lips, did they stick out? My skin, was it smooth? Had I applied my make-up properly this morning? I had never been that good at it and I was only allowed a few bits and pieces by my aunt. I'm the impatient type and get easily frustrated when something requires time and precision. At that moment I wished I had learnt to be a little more careful when it comes to make-up. Never mind, I thought, I'm sure I'll learn at lot here.

I hoped that the Queen liked my choice of dress and accessories. I had chosen a deep red dress with matching shoes, necklace, earrings and handbag. I felt an ache inside of me, desperately wanting her approval. As if she could read my thoughts, the Queen – who up to this point seemed to have been unaware of my presence – turned to face me. Accordingly, every girl turned their bodies towards me. The familiar look of the Reachables faced me. They stared at me blankly, yet with a condescending attitude. Their unspoken message was clear, *You aren't as beautiful as us, or as perfect. We are so much better than you.*

Memories of my life in the valley filled me. I remembered how I had hated their stares. Did I really want to become like them? Perhaps it would be different if I was one of them? The Queen straightened herself up and then addressed me in a softer, yet strained voice,

'Oh, yes, you girl. I had almost forgotten that you would come today. Time for you to decide, isn't it? What do you think of my beauties? You see what I have to offer you, child. You too can be like them. You can leave behind all your imperfection, walk out of the shadows and come into my wonderful light.'

A knot wrenched inside my stomach and waves of nausea hit me. She had caught me, exposed the deep longing in my heart. The girls around her raised their eyebrows, narrowed their eyes and smirked at me in unison. It was clear that they despised me for not reaching up to their standards. Suddenly my whole being ached to become part of this chosen group. The Queen's eyes narrowed and a frown appeared on her forehead.

'You have made your decision, child, I hope. I don't have time to waste, you know.'

Just seconds before I had been unsure as to what I would reply, but now in her presence I felt sure.

'Yes, Your Majesty, I have decided and I want to become part of your kingdom … your family,' I added hesitantly.

'Excellent, you have chosen wisely and just as I had planned. Now we must get to work immediately.' She clapped her hands forcefully and turned to the young girl closest to her.

'You know the drill, get her fixed up and don't forget the most important thing.'

I was torn between great excitement and fear. Would I finally become what I had always longed for? But what would happen with my mind?

First, I was taken to an enormous bathroom where I was scrubbed down with an array of intoxicating oils and lotions. Then, a whole crew of girls entered and each one was assigned different tasks. Some attended to my face, others my clothes, my hair and so on. It took hours. But slowly a transformation began to take place. It was invigorating, wonderful and agonising. No one talked to me during the whole time which was sad, but I comforted myself with the belief that they would most certainly become my friends after I had undergone the transformation.

After hours of preparation my body felt worn and bruised. I was allowed to look in the mirror and there was no denying that I looked amazing, just like any Reachable I had met in the valley. I was happy but something bothered me. I had never imagined that so much time and pain would be involved. Surely I wouldn't have to go through this everyday?

My mouth was dry and my stomach rumbled. I turned to the girls.

'Will we be getting anything to eat or drink?' I begged. 'I'm very hungry and I feel quite weak.'

The three girls working on me at the time smirked back at me. They looked at each other fleetingly as if they held a secret. I heard one whisper to the other.

'Should we tell her, she has made her decision after all?'

'I guess it won't harm her to know now. Better that she understands what she's getting herself into.' They turned to me and spoke,

'You are part of the Queen's kingdom now. You might as well get used to these feelings. We are all on a strict diet here. We are not allowed more than 500 calories a day and we are all carefully monitored, obviously no one is allowed to become fat in the Queen's kingdom. She determines what *fat* is.'

They looked at each other again and whispered,

'Every morning we are weighed and we all live in constant fear that we will overstep the measurements. If that should ever happen, you will be instantly removed from this place … forever.'

I was shocked to hear their confession. The Queen hadn't mentioned anything about this. Admittedly, they did leave me to starve the first few days but as soon as I was moved to my special bedroom they had been feeding me well. And if I thought about it, all the food I had been served so far had been salads and fruit, but I hadn't been left to feel hungry, not like this. Still, I shook off their words. In fact they were partly encouraging. Wasn't this exactly how I had lived before I was taken to the Cave. Wasn't that what I had decided, that I would beat my body into obedience. No, this will be prefect. I have no desire to become fat either. In fact, when I think about it, I thought I was looking fatter this morning when I looked in the large mirror in my new bedroom. It doesn't matter that I feel weak and hungry – it's good for me, very good.

Once they were done with my appearance, they took me back to my bedroom and told me to wait until I'm called again. I've been here for a few hours now and I wonder when they will come for me? I'm bored and I feel lonely in this place. Even though I'm all dressed up and looking beautiful, there is no one to see me or share it with.

Day 44

Dear Diary,

Let me tell you all that has happened. They took me along a wide corridor to a large bronze door. There was a sign outside it that read, *The Correction Room*. I wondered what that meant. There was so much that still needed correcting in my body and perhaps the solution lay behind these doors. The doorknob turned and a yet another girl opened it for me. She motioned for me to enter. The two girls who had led me this far looked fearfully at each other and ran off, back down the corridor we had just come through.

I looked tentatively around the room and was surprised to see so many mirrors. They were all over the walls, ceiling and even on the floor. It was a strange sensation to be surrounded by reflections of yourself wherever you looked. Never before had I been confronted with such an image of 'self'. I should have enjoyed looking at myself from all these different angles after all the work that had been done on my appearance in the past few hours, but I could hardly bring myself to look. When I finally did I felt no joy or pride, just emptiness.

Towards the centre of the room, I saw a sinister-looking black chair. Memories of visits to the dentist rushed through my mind. Especially this one time when the dentist had to fix a hole in a molar and needed to drill deep into my root canal. He had refused to give me anything for the pain and the whole experience had been very traumatic and painful. I shuddered just thinking about it and felt a sudden ache in that tooth. There was a machine next to the chair. It had two buttons on it, one green and one red, and it was connected to a devise which appeared to be designed for the human head. I began to wonder what I had got myself into.

I began to contemplate my escape routes when, suddenly, the Queen appeared out of nowhere with a number of Reachables. She stood between me and the door, which was the only way out that I could see. When I saw her I was taken aback and gasped in surprise. The Queen that stood before me looked quite different from the one I had met this morning. Her face was taut and hard and her eyes were no longer blue but black and filled with hate and anger. She looked me up and down with a cold and unmerciful stare and then spoke,

'Good, I am glad to see that the girls have been able to work on you. You are far from perfect, but still so much better than before. Now is the time to relinquish the right to your own mind, my child. Remember your side of the bargain.'

The Queen's reflection could be seen on all the mirrors in the room and I felt trapped and sensed I was in great danger. Sweat appeared on my hands and a cold chill went down my spine. I knew that I had agreed to this, but …

The large, black chair stood before me.

'Sit down, girl!' the Queen commanded.

Jumping to her command I sat down but my body shook with fear as a sense of impending doom washed over me. I tried to convince myself that it was worth it for the sake of beauty. What was my mind anyway? Just a collection of thoughts and memories and dreams. Did I really need it?

The Queen pointed to the other girls in the room and three of them tied my legs and arms firmly to the chair. I heard a humming noise above me and saw the metal helmet lowering down towards my heard. When it touched the top of my head it snapped down, covering me completely in a firm grip. I winced as the girls tightened the screws in place. Excruciating pain shot through my brain and I cried out,

'Stop it, you are hurting me!'

I looked over at the Queen, pleading for a second chance. She seemed oblivious to my pain and pleadings and simply stated,

'Say goodbye to your past, child, and welcome your future. A future without wrinkle or blemish. In only half an hour, your mind will be mine, to own and control. Welcome to the world of the Reachables and to my kingdom.'

In a split second the full realisation of what I had done hit me and I knew that I had made a terrible mistake. I was gripped with panic and tried to move but it was too late.

Helplessly, I watched as the Queen turned to push the green button. Electric shock waves shot through my head and images flashed through my mind. As I saw them in my mind's eye, they were simultaneously displayed on the mirrors in the room. My childhood, visits to the hairdressers, my school friends, my father, my history teacher, the bakery, vomiting … I was surrounded by these pictures and overcome. In the midst of it when I felt like I could not take it anymore I called out,

'Father, father, help me! I know I've chosen the wrong path. Give me one more chance. I choose you. I choose the route of freedom.' I felt as if my mind would explode and then, suddenly, it all ended.

The next thing I saw was Gentle's face. He stood beside the red button which he had just pushed. The sound of screams and sirens filled the room. Shocked and dizzy I made out Gentle's face in front of me. The look on his face was resolute and yet as he looked at me tears streamed down his cheeks. Before I had time to register anything else, he released the switches on the chair and the locks around my arms, legs and head, and I was free. I felt his strong arms lift me up and my body relaxed. I looked into his eyes and heard him, with anguish in his voice, ask me,

'What have you done? Why did you take this step?'

'I'm so sorry,' was all I could answer.

At Gentle's appearance the girls around us began to change in front of our eyes. They were no longer sweet and beautiful. Cracks appeared on their foreheads, their skin became like scales on a crocodile, broken, uneven. Suddenly, they became the Creatures I had seen in the valley and I saw them for who they really were …

The Queen let out a piercing scream behind me,

'Don't let her get away. Don't let her see the girls like that. Quick, call the stewardesses. I demand that they do their magic now!'

But it was too late, I had already realised that the Reachables were no longer something to be desired. Their beauty was only an illusion, a cover for something terrible underneath. As Gentle carried me away I looked back at the transformed girls in the room and as they stood before me I saw their contorted lips mouthing out,

'Help us! Please help us!'

I heard the words echo in the air – *'Help us!'* – and their cry seemed to be joined with the voices of thousands of girls crying out in unison. I thought of all those girls that I had seen around the Queen's throne earlier that day and wondered what would happen to them now. A large eagle appeared and lifted me and Gentle onto its wings and flew us out of the Queen's kingdom, back to the Cave.

Evening

My mind is clearing up the longer I'm out of the Queen's realm. The purity and freshness of the air here is a welcome contrast to the intoxicating and seductive atmosphere in her kingdom. They placed me in the emergency room where I've been all afternoon. Doctors checked my pulse, my body and my brain.

'Most can be salvaged. We hope that the most important things have not been lost,' I heard them discuss. 'The dreams could have been removed from her, the training. We don't know yet.'

Allister sat beside me the whole time and held my hand, whilst Gentle sat in the far corner, his head faced downwards. Allister looked at me, his eyes moist and tender. I dared not speak to him, I felt so ashamed. Finally, he broke the uncomfortable silence,

'Abisha, I know you must be wondering about what happened. Why we didn't try to stop the Creatures from taking you? This may be hard for you to understand, but we had no other choice than to let you go. You had to face your own fears, connect with your deepest longing and finally make a choice about what you ultimately desire for your life. The Eternal Law required it. The Queen knew that after your 18th birthday, you were legally responsible for your own life and were allowed to make your own decisions. We were bound by the law from helping you. You needed to experience for yourself the emptiness of what the Queen was offering you, and to see the Reachables for who they truly are.'

He sighed and then squeezed my hand, as if to encourage me, then continued,

'You must rest, eat a little and strengthen yourself. There are many who are relying on you and without your determination, right now, we will not make it through.'

'But, I don't understand. I chose to go with the Queen, I allowed her to make me over: the hair, the make-up and …' I could barely speak at this point, '… even my mind. If the law forbade you to help me, why did you come to my rescue once I was there?'

'When it came to surrendering your mind to her, you resisted.' Allister said, with great emphasis. 'You knew deep inside that it was wrong and your heart reacted. When you called out to your father for help – it was at that moment that the law was broken and we were instantly released to come and rescue you.'

'But how could you come so quickly, how did you know where I was?'

'We were with you all the time. We were watching and standing outside your door. We saw you and desperately wanted to reach out and speak to you. To comfort you, but we could not. All we could do was to watch, wait and hope.'

'But I didn't see you at all, I didn't feel you. I felt all alone.'

'We were there, you were not able to see us, but we were there.'

'I feel as if I've failed you all and … myself. I didn't resist her temptations. I doubted you in that place and began to see you and Gentle as the enemy. I thought that you had betrayed me and I was so angry with you. Everything was so foggy. Dream and reality became mixed-up for me. I'm so sorry.' I poured out my heart in desperation, almost unable to bring myself to finish.

'Don't accuse yourself Abisha,' Allister replied kindly. 'I know that right now it appears as if you've failed, but the experience that you've just had was necessary. You needed to fully comprehend what the Queen's kingdom represents. How can you fight something that you do not understand? It was vital for you to see what she's truly like. Most of all, you needed to see the girls with your own eyes. See behind their facade to who they really are. I knew that day would come even when we first brought you to the Cave.'

'But, Allister,' I asked, hardly daring to utter the question. 'Was it wrong to long for the beauty, the clothes, everything that the Queen offered me? My heart came alive when I saw those things and I desperately wanted to have them.'

'No, it is not wrong to long for those things, and it is not wrong to want to be beautiful. What you needed to learn and will soon understand is that all those extras that the Queen offered you are not necessary for you to obtain true beauty. She offered you something you already possess. You are beautiful, you always have been. It is time for you to enter the door.'

I instantly knew he meant the door that had intrigued and scared me when I first came to the Cave.

They led me there straight away and Gentle placed a comforting hand on my shoulder as we walked, sensing how nervous I was.

When we arrived I looked up at the door and it appeared larger and more daunting than ever. It was made of solid oak with inscriptions on it from an alphabet I didn't recognise. I stared at the door, knowing it was time to enter but not knowing how. Allister stood beside me and gave me a reassuring nudge saying,

'You can do it, Abisha. This door is prepared for you. Just open it.'

I took a step towards it and looked to see if Gentle was going to follow me, but he remained at the doorpost and appeared neither willing nor able to follow me inside the room.

What struck me first was the mirror in the left hand corner of the room. It was alive, much like the waterfall in the village square. Movement came from within, mysterious and welcoming. This mirror drew me by invitation, rather than by threat. Somehow I knew that this was a mirror that I could trust. I moved slowly towards it, took a deep breath and looked into it. I jumped back in shock. I didn't recognise the girl who stood before me.

My hair was silky and flowing just as my father's in his photo. My face was perfect and my complexion soft. My lips were delicately formed and nothing to be ashamed of. My body was not the same, not what I had seen before. It was perfectly proportioned. There were no bits sticking out. I looked long and hard for the slightest imperfection, for a trace of something to correct. But in this place and in front of that mirror it was impossible to find anything wrong. There was no denying it. I am beautiful and I am not fat.

Suddenly, the mirror spoke in a voice that reminded me of the waves of the ocean,

'Abisha, this is how you've always looked, you were created this way. The mirrors you've beheld your whole life are the Queen's creation. She has programmed them to reflect what she wants you to see. They present an image that is full of deception and lies.' The mirror continued,

'The Queen tried to offer you something that you already owned. Her offer was no offer at all, only a trick to take you captive in her kingdom. It is the same offer she makes to the people in the valley. She controls the minds of the people there, creates an image of perfection that does not exist in reality. Every person you've known as a Reachable is in fact a Creature that she has created. Take a good look at yourself and be free. You are perfect.'

The realisation that, all along, I had possessed what I thought I could never own was sickening as much as it was liberating. I am not fat and I am not ugly. What is fat? What is ugly? Words that haunt every girl I know. So much wasted time and energy spent by all of us trying to correct something that does not exist.

At first I was relieved, but now I'm angry. How she has deceived us, this Queen. I think of all my friends, back in the valley, both girls and guys, who have been trapped for so many years. They own the right to be free. Someone must let them know – I want to find them and show each one of them this mirror.

I ran out of the room, and before I could say anything to Allister he said,

'I know Abisha, I've always seen you like that. Finally you see.'

I wanted to return to the valley straight away but Allister said I must wait.

'You need to recover first and complete your training. When the time is right we will act.'

I knew he was right, but all I want is to give others the freedom I feel right now.

Day 45

I'm slowly recovering. The shock of the Queen's kingdom is starting to sink in, as is the severity of the situation. I keep thinking about those girls and their cry for help haunts me as I hear it echoing in my mind. The thought of all those thousands of girls trapped in her trickery is tragic.

Today, Allister explained some of the Queen's history to me.

'The Queen was born together with her twin sister to a frontier couple who were among the most gentle and faithful people in the Cave. The sisters were identical twins and their parents loved them both dearly.

When the Queen was 5 years old tragedy struck. The family's home was destroyed by an earthquake. Her parents and her sister were able to get out of the house in time but the Queen, deep in sleep, had not heard their cries and was trapped inside as the house caved in around her. The girl's sweet face was destroyed and her body mauled beyond recognition.

Doctors were called in from all over the land to try to help and she underwent numerous operations attempting to restore her face but none were fully successful, for the damage was extensive. Her parents continued to love her as before despite her change in appearance, as did her sister, but the Queen was never the same after that. She could not accept her marred appearance and began to be filled with bitterness and hate. She shut her parents and sister out and no matter how much love and acceptance they poured out on her, she rejected them and pushed them away.

Things became worse when the Queen started school at the age of six. None of the other children wanted to play with her and would tease her whenever she stepped into a room. Wherever she walked, people would point fingers at her and let out gasps of horror and disgust. A sensitive child, they said, and she would often be found weeping at every break at school. Her twin sister – who was as beautiful as the Queen had once been – increased in popularity in school and the Queen started to resent her and became insanely jealous of her.

The Queen's life was wrecked and filled with pain and rejection which increased the older she became. Rumours say that she turned to food to comfort herself and, as the years went on, became larger and larger. She was now taunted not only for her scars but for her increased weight. It was not unusual for cries like *Fatty!* and *Blubber girl!* to be shouted at her as she walked down the street.

This suffering continued until her 14th birthday and then took her life into her own hands and things began to change drastically. People started noticing that she grew thinner and thinner until there was almost nothing left of her. Whereas before she had been the object of taunts, she now channelled the accusations over to others. The victim became the victimizer. Her class was terrified of her and her reputation went before her in the valley. It was reported that when she came into the classroom, a dark mist would cover the room and those around her would be paralysed with fear. She ruled the room with her aggression and no one was safe. Her anger was specifically targeted towards the girls in the valley and especially her sister. Harshness and bitterness consumed her and her heart froze like ice. Those who had once been able to cause her much pain were now petrified of her. One glance from her eye could slice them to pieces. Known as the *Ice Girl*, she breathed death and fear on everyone.

On her 20th birthday, the Queen disappeared and was never seen in the valley again. Her parents searched everywhere for her, but never found her. They were devastated to loose their daughter in so many ways.

A few years after her disappearance, the Mirror took over the valley. Laughter was replaced by fear, kindness with mistrust and freedom with its control. The Mirror established a set of rules that could not be found anywhere else. It was then that the Reachable force, who were to keep these rules in place, appeared. The mirrors appeared at the same time, shipped in scores and placed in every home and by every street corner.

The concept fat was introduced. People were placed into different categories, depending on their weight and outside appearance. Young girls were specifically targeted. Messages were communicated, day and night: *You are not good enough, not beautiful, not lovely.* Beauty now had a face. A list of prerequisites were introduced and written out as a set of measurements. The shape of your nose, lips, forehead was what counted. Hair, a certain length and style. No diversions from the norm allowed. Weight was carefully monitored and anyone who did not conform was to be punished verbally and emotionally. Life in the valley was transformed into a prison.'

When Allister had finished telling me all about the Queen's history, I sat shocked for some time. So much of her story reminded me of my own battle and experiences in the valley. Pieces of a puzzle started to fall into place as I realised some of the background to the place where I had grown up and spent all my life. I can't understand why no one in the valley knows about the Queen. There, no one fully knows where the mirrors came from, but the People of the Cave do. They understand the connection between the Queen and the Mirror and have devised a plan to overcome them both. I seem to be at the very centre of that plan.

Day 46

I dreamt again last night. The girls from the Queen's throne room were gathered around me in a circle. Their mouths were taped over and their arms tied with ropes behind their backs. Their muffled screams penetrated the night air. I knew they were calling my name. But I could not understand what they expected of me? What can I do to help them?

The dream disturbed me so much that I went to talk to Allister about it as soon as I woke up. He listened and then spoke tenderly to me,

'Don't fear the voices. You will help those girls, and many others, when the time is right. We will explain everything soon. Your focus now must be on getting yourself well. Learn to love and to accept all parts of yourself. Your mind has been programmed by the Mirror for a long time and you must allow it to be re-trained. We will not act as the Queen did. She wanted your mind in order to control you, but we simply want to help you to be free from the lies of the past that have tormented you. We are on your side Abisha, please trust that and never doubt us again.'

His words soothed me and I felt relieved that Allister doesn't seem to be angry with me after my time with the Queen. I cannot imagine anything worse than him withdrawing from me.

After our talk and breakfast, Gentle and Allister took me to a room at the far end of the Cave that I had never seen before. When I entered the room it looked like a large auditorium and reminded me of a movie theatre. There was a huge screen in front of me and a row of seats that adjusted to your shape as you sat in them. Allister directed me to a chair in the centre of the front row. He sat to my left and Gentle to my right.

Scenes from my past were presented on the screen and for each scene a word was written across it. I saw myself at the moment of my birth and the word Chosen One was written across my forehead. Then I came to a scene showing the first five years of my life. I saw the words *Loved* and *Cared For*. Then I saw a scene from when I was 10 years old, and the words *Afraid*, *Unlovely* and *Worthless* appeared. It felt as if someone had slapped me across the face. I had lived my whole life in the shadow of those words.

Suddenly the screen split in two: I could see the old messages that I had lived through on the left side, but at the same time, other messages appeared on the right. I saw the words *Brave*, *Messenger* and *Overcomer*. I didn't understand. Where were those words coming from? Could they be true? I looked over at Allister, wanting him to explain what was going on. He said,

'What you see before you, Abisha, is the complexity of your life. Certain messages were implanted in you, but they were not true. Now you have a chance to see things as they really are. The messages on the left are the lies the Queen wanted you to believe. She has always been after your mind, to control you. The messages that appear on the right are your true identity, the words of your father. Now you're being shown the whole picture and you can choose. Will you agree with her words or the words of your father?'

I looked at myself as a 10-year-old again and decided to embrace the messages on the right: *I am brave. I am a messenger. I am an overcomer.* As I did, a flash appeared before my eyes and I felt my mind change. I looked again and to my surprise the old messages had disappeared. The words that had caused me so much pain were gone and their power and influence broken.

We spent the morning going through the scenes of my life. Every time I chose from the right, I was transformed. I feel as if my brain is being reprogrammed. I get to choose, I get to decide and I'm embracing a new identity. I'm finding out who I truly am.

Day 47

Dear Diary,

It's not enough to feel free myself – I know that I must help those trapped in the valley and even the servants of the Queen. I need to walk on the path as the Messenger, as the Chosen One. Now that my mind has been renewed, Gentle told me, I must continue with my training.

Allister supervised me today as Gentle apparently was needed for something urgent. I found it hard to concentrate on using my sword and shield while Allister was around. I'm sure he feels it too. There is something between us. It both confuses and excites me. Despite all the transformation of yesterday I still find it hard to believe that any guy could want to be around me, let alone love me. Perhaps I'm just making it up. I would never dare to tell him how I feel in case he doesn't feel the same. It's really not the right time to be thinking about things like this anyway, we have so much to do.

I found the training hard, and after a week in the Queen's kingdom my arms are weaker. The sword is the hardest to master because it's so heavy. My arms ached as I lifted it up in the air.

'Higher, higher!' Allister shouted. 'You can't expect to defeat the Queen from that position, dear one.'

When he said, *dear one*, I felt patronised and the only feeling I had towards him then was anger. I'm not just a little girl that he can boss around, even if he seems to know more than me in this area. If he wants me to fight, I'll show him. After that I really improved as the adrenalin rushed through my body. He didn't call me *dear one* again, but seemed to be pleased that I made such progress. I wonder if he had even said it on purpose just to provoke me? I wanted to give up so many times today, but I managed to keep going until late in the afternoon.

Besides my feelings for Allister, I've noticed something else today. There is a lot of movement in the Cave. Troops have been marching back and forth all day. Something seems to be going on and I know that I heard Mr Sann's name mentioned four times at lunch. I don't understand why they would be talking about him here and now? Allister refused to answer my prying questions when I talked to him about it at dinner.

'It's not for you to know, not yet anyway …' is all he would say when I tried to ask him.

I'm glad I persevered through my training today though, one step closer to helping others.

Day 48

I didn't need to wait long to find out what all of yesterday's activity was about – Mr Sann is here! Two of the people in the Cave found him in the valley, left for dead by the fountain. He lay there beaten, bloodied and barely conscious. He is to be debriefed later today, but first he's being checked by the medical team, not only for his wounds, but also for possible bugs implanted by the Mirror. He must undergo a dangerous operation to be sure.

'We can never be too careful,' I overheard Allister say to Gentle. 'We are of course relieved to have him back, but we can't endanger the rest of the Cave and definitely not the Messenger,' he continued.

I asked for permission to watch as the doctors worked with Mr Sann and only after much persistence did they allow me. They poured a special oil into his wounds and as it touched his broken body, a wonderful transformation took place. The torn skin disappeared, the blood dried up and soft, plump, fresh skin appeared. As the oil touched his face, it penetrated every taught line and the strain and trace of trauma that was so evident when he first arrived evaporated into the air. It was as if ten years had been taken off his face and the kind history teacher I had grown to admire was restored before my eyes.

Allister said that what was to happen next could be unpleasant for me to see, but I insisted on staying. He turned to Mr Sann and with anguish in his voice beyond anything I had never heard before said,

'You know what we must do next. We must be sure. Do we have your permission, Father?'

When he spoke the word *father*, it was if something I had suspected all along fell into place. That's why I sensed such a strong bond between them in the valley.

Mr Sann met his gaze and with tears pouring down his face agreed,

'It is the only way, my son. Do it now and don't be afraid. I will make it through this, I am sure.'

'Yes, Father, it is for the common good.' Allister choked out his reply.

They proceeded to cut open Mr Sann's brain. The last thing I remembered was that my insides retched and everything went fuzzy before my eyes. The next thing I knew I was sitting on a chair outside the room with a blanket around me and Gentle was offering me a cup of sweetened tea. I was angry with myself for fainting. It was the blood that did it, I could never stand the sight of it.

'How did it go? Did they find anything inside his mind?' I pleaded with Gentle, desperate to know what the outcome had been. Gentle made me finish my tea first before he agreed to fetch Allister who began to fill me in on the details.

'My father is safe. He has survived the operation,' he uttered. 'The Queen was not able to implant anything. The doctors have applied their oil and he is healing and resting now. The debriefing will take place tomorrow.'

Relief washed over me and I wanted to sink into Allister's arms when he asked, 'How are you?'

But again my words failed me and all I could get out was,

'I'm fine. I'm so sorry, I didn't know Mr Sann was your father. Are you okay?'

'I'm all right. I'm so happy to have my father home again, but even without him I would keep on fighting. I was born into this assignment. You and I share a common destiny. Our fathers worked to liberate others. They fought for freedom and so must we.'

He spoke like a true hero. He is so selfless and brave. I wish I could be more like him.

Day 49

After a good night of rest for all of us, it was time for Mr Sann's debriefing and I was allowed to sit in on it. He was fully restored and no trace could be seen of the ordeal he had been through or the scars from the surgery. The oil they use to heal is amazing. The embarrassing thing was that before they began, Mr Sann turned to me and with eyes filled with love and concern, he said,

'It's so wonderful to see you in this place, Abisha. You are the reason that I came to the valley and I'm relieved that you made it here safely.'

I hugged him, thanking him for risking his life for me.

'How can I ever repay you?' I asked.

'Stand as the Messenger and complete your assignment,' was his reply. Mr Sann seemed to neither care for his health, nor the ordeal that he had been through. It was clear that he lived for a greater purpose, higher than himself. He turned to the others in the room and spoke,

'My friends, we are all in great danger. The Queen has sent out her spies and she has become even more sophisticated in her ways. It appears that the worst has befallen us … traitors. There are those among us who are not who they appear to be. We must be on our guard. It is a great tragedy. The band of trust has been broken. This was how they were able to capture me.'

The look of shock on everyone's face was contagious and some cried out,

'Traitors amongst us? This cannot be!'

Mr Sann took charge and kept on talking,

'We knew that this could happen,' he said. 'We allow choice in this place and all are free to choose the way of the Mirror rather than work for freedom here in the Cave. We have prepared ourselves for this day, even though we hoped it would never come. Now we must be realistic. It is neither time for fear, nor time to back down.'

'How many do you think are affected?' Allister asked his father.

'We don't know, but we must be prepared for the worst. It's time to put the Heart Serum into action. It was prepared for this and we must eliminate the threat immediately,' Mr Sann hastily replied.

'Abisha must be protected at all costs. Take her to the safe place immediately. She must go to the Glass Room. Now!'

Glass Room? I had no idea what they were talking about but I knew that I had no choice but to follow them. The realisation that the Queen had infiltrated our ranks was devastating. Immediately, I was whisked away and yet again I was so thankful that I carry you around with me everywhere I go.

The Glass Room that Gentle took me to is wonderful. Exquisite light fills the room, surrounded with beautiful glass walls, connected into each other. They glisten as the sea as light hits them from different angles, shifting between pearl, turquoise and amber. There is a small white bed in the left corner of the room. The bedspread is magnificent with images of flowers in varying shades of creams and whites. Next to the bed there is a reading desk with four books on top of it. Two are history books, similar to the one that Mr Sann gave me, one is filled with beautiful pictures and the fourth one is called *The Heart of the Father*. The last one beckoned to me. Instinctively I knew that if I were to look inside it, my life would never be the same. There are no lights or candles in the room as the reflections from the glass provide all the light needed.

'How long do I need to stay here?' I wondered.

'As long as it is necessary,' Allister replied. 'Read everything you want to here. I must return to my father now.'

Then he left me and now I'm stuck here alone and it is frustrating. I can see a great deal of activity from inside these walls of glass. Soldiers run past me, two, three at a time. I don't know why they put me here and why I can't be a part of the action. Allister promised to visit me later to explain what is going on, so for now I'll just have to stay put.

Evening

The worst has happened and I'm devastated.

As promised, Allister came to visit me, bringing me my evening meal. His eyes were red and swollen. He looked like he carried the weight of many troubles on his shoulders.

'Eat, Abisha. You need it.' He looked at me sternly when I tried to protest, saying that I wasn't hungry. I knew that this was non-negotiable and I ate every last bite. Chicken pie with vegetables and potatoes. Strange that you often don't realise how hungry you are until you start eating.

'Are you all right, Allister?' I asked once I had eaten. 'You look so pale. What is going on? Can I help?'

It shocked me to realise that it was only when I had taken care of my own needs that I had the energy and focus to care about others. My selfishness over the past few weeks caused me to wince with shame and I was determined to make a change.

'There's little that you can do at this point, Abisha,' was all he could utter. 'We must find the traitor and remove him or her from this place. My father is searching desperately amongst the soldiers and everyone must take the Heart Serum as a test. It is such a waste of our precious Serum but we have no other choice. Until the traitor is found all of our plans and strategies must be brought to a standstill. We cannot afford to take any risks at all, especially not with you here.'

'But why am I locked up in this room? Why can't I help you out there?' I wondered.

'We must ensure that no one hears what we tell you, and we can't risk that the traitor would try to speak to you,' he replied wearily. 'This is the safest place in the Cave, built by your father just for these types of eventualities. He would often spend his days and nights in this room. It was here that he wrote his books and finished his last book, *The Heart of the Father.* Your father was a great scholar. He was loved by his friends, known for his gentleness and kindness, and respected and feared by his enemies for his insight and fearlessness. Writing that last book was a great battle for him. He spent days and weeks pacing the floor of this room, looking for answers and ways to articulate his thoughts.'

'I was a young boy at the time,' Allister added, 'and I would slip out from my morning classes and sit and watch your father as he worked and wrote. He intrigued me and I was drawn to his passion and depth.

You remind me of him in many ways. You have his resilience and …'

He paused to think and a grin appeared on his face as he concluded, 'his stubbornness.'

I was proud to be compared to my father who seemed to have been such a great man, but was not as excited about the stubborn part.

'Tell me more about my father,' I pleaded, desperate to find out more about him. The thought that he had been in this very room years ago moved me and made me feel connected to him. I longed to reach out and touch him and so wished that he was here with me now, to be held by him. Even now as a young woman, a place deep inside of me called out for the father I'd hardly known.

'There is no time now,' was Allister's disappointing reply. 'I know that you have many questions and that you want to understand, but these are dark days. I'm tired, and there's a lot weighing on my heart right now. As much as I would like to, now is not the time.'

I was ashamed of my selfishness again, I had forgotten the problem at hand and become caught up in my own longings.

'Yes, I understand. I'm sorry, please continue. What did you come to tell me,' I quickly replied.

'We need to evacuate the training rooms and the school must also come to a standstill. We cannot have the traitors, whoever they are, learning more about our secrets and we must keep the children protected. They are one of our greatest treasures and nothing must reach them to corrupt them. There's to be a great gathering tomorrow morning. The true purpose of the meeting hasn't been revealed at this point. We have said that we are gathering to discuss our new strategy against the Queen. That should ensure us that the traitor will be present as they would not want to miss such vital information.'

'Can I be there?' I asked hesitantly, not sure at this point what Allister would allow.

'Yes, you must be present, otherwise the traitor may suspect that something is wrong. Just be careful, very careful. Don't say anything to anyone. No matter who may approach you. Trust nobody, not at this stage,' he sighed.

A terrible thought crossed my mind and I saw that he noticed and guessed what I was thinking.

'You wonder if you can trust me?' he voiced the awful question for me.

'Yes, I uh, I'm sorry,' I stumbled. 'It's not that I don't want to, it's just when you said that I must not trust anyone.'

'It is all right, I understand,' he replied kindly. 'These are difficult times and we are forced to ask hard questions.'

'I thought you might ask me this and I brought a vial of the Heart Serum with me. I've already taken it with my father and the other leaders as they were forced to question even me. My father looked me in the eye as soon as we discovered about the traitor and with tears in his eyes said, "My precious son, I am sorry to announce that you must be the first to take the Serum. You know that I trust you, but in these days we cannot take any chances." But now I'm getting ahead of myself,' Allister sighed again.

He took the small glass vial out of his bag. It glistened much like the walls of the Glass Room we found ourselves in. He showed me the contents.

'This is the Serum. We need another witness who can explain the process and monitor the results.'

He pushed a green button on the wall and the first glass door opened up. Gentle was waiting outside, patiently and silently. I had not seen him, but my instinct told me he had been there all along. Allister called him in and nodded.

'You know the process, Gentle. Explain to Abisha how it works and then I'll take it.'

Gentle turned towards me and said,

'Just watch as Allister takes the Serum now. If you see light emanate from his eyes, then you know that he is pure. But, if his eyes become black after taking the Serum, you know that the heart of a traitor resides inside of him.'

I wasn't really worried as I knew that Allister had already taken the Serum with his father and the leaders and passed. He took a sip of the Serum and we waited for the expected light to shine from his eyes. And then it happened. The pupils in Allister's eyes narrowed and then the whole eye turned black. A thought shot through my mind – *I must be dreaming. This can't be happening.* We all let out a scream of terror, but Allister's was the worst of all.

'NOOOO,' he screamed. 'Someone has set me up! I am no traitor, you know that Abisha, Gentle?'

He turned to look at us, desperately imploring us to listen. But as he spoke his eyes only darkened and we didn't know what to believe. I fell to the floor in horror and covered my eyes as I couldn't bear to look at him anymore. Those eyes that I had so grown to love and which had brought me so much comfort were now filled with a deathly coldness that I recognised from my time with the Queen. Gentle also appeared to be in total shock and stood motionless.

Allister lowered his gaze as he turned to Gentle and with a quivering voice spoke,

'You must both let me go. You know this isn't as it seems. I am no traitor. Someone has tricked me. Please let me go now and I'll find the one responsible. Trust me, I'm my father's child and I would never betray my people. I've laid down my life for the cause and nothing would stop me from fulfilling my duty. If you would both trust me, I promise to search for the one responsible. If you hand me in now, then the true traitor has won and will only continue in his deceit. I will ask you one final time, please trust me.'

His words cut through our shock and Gentle and I exchanged hesitant glances. For what seemed like hours, we both contemplated Allister's words. Finally, Gentle spoke,

'I've known and watched over you since you were a child, Allister. I know you have a noble heart. I do not understand what we see before us, but I do trust who I know you to be. I'll let you go until after the meeting tomorrow morning but if you do not appear with an explanation before that time, we will be forced to speak of what we have seen here today. Run, quickly and hide. We will not speak of these things and we trust that truth will lead you. Run before the guards appear and see you.'

I couldn't look Allister in the eye. As he turned to walk out of the door he whispered,

'Abisha, I may never see you again and you may never trust me again but please know that I ... I uh ... I.'

He stuttered out the last words and seemed unable to finish his sentence. And then, just as I turned to him and hoped that he would speak the words I longed to hear, he was gone. Into the recesses of the Cave and now I no longer care if I live or die. It was at that point that I knew that the man who had just walked out was the man that I loved.

In the trauma of the moment Gentle was my only comfort. 'Come here, child,' was all he needed to say. I ran to him and fell into his arms, strong, secure and loving, and I wept. Once I had calmed down a bit Gentle said,

'I don't understand how this could happen but I know Allister and I know he is no traitor. He will find the ones responsible, I'm sure of that. Until then, speak of this to no one. We will continue with the meeting as planned. I'll fetch you tomorrow morning after breakfast. We must not disclose our distress.'

And with those words he left me, although I know he is close by.

Now you know, my dear Diary, and there are no more words for me to write or tears left to cry.

Day 50

My dreams were troubled again last night. Images of Allister's black eyes, the Heart Serum, shattered mirrors and the Queen flashed intermittently before my eyes. My relief at waking up was short-lived as I realised that reality was just as dreadful. Today was also a strange and unnerving experience.

Gentle came to fetch me in the morning. Neither of us mentioned what had happened last night but our bloodshot, heavy eyes spoke for us. I slipped my hand into his and he squeezed it tightly.

We walked into the Assembly Hall and saw row upon row of soldiers lined up in front of us. Dressed in their golden uniforms they looked magnificent and intimidating. Standing perfectly still, the only sign that they were alive was the occasional movement from their chests as they breathed in and out. Each held a sword in his right hand and a shield in his left. Their eyes looked straight ahead towards the platform on which Mr Sann was standing. He was surrounded by the other leaders. He motioned for Gentle and me to join them on the stage and reluctantly we moved towards them. He greeted me with a warm hug and then asked the inevitable,

'Have you seen Allister anywhere today? I've searched everywhere for him but he seems to have disappeared.'

I could feel my cheeks redden as I stuttered out my reply,

'No, I uh, haven't seen him today. I'm sure he will be here any minute. He said he was very tired last night so I'm sure he's on his way.'

Gentle caught my gaze, nodded his head and added,

'Don't worry, Mr Sann. You know your son. We can trust him. He will be here soon and, I'm sure, give a good explanation.'

My heart beat wildly and I felt light-headed. I needed to sit down – fast. Gentle gripped hold of my hand and steadied me. He helped me to the nearest chair and pulled his own close to mine. Having him there beside me kept me from bursting into tears and ruining everything.

The meeting was called to a start and a trumpet blown. A shell-shaped instrument which let out a distinct, eerie sound that resounded throughout the Cave. Surely Allister must have heard it? Would he show up, I wondered.

Mr Sann took centre stage and addressed the Servants of the Court.

'I've gathered you here today with a heavy heart. As you know, I was recently captured by the Queen and her troops. She was unsuccessful in her attempts to expose us. But …'

I noticed how his voice began to falter at this point and became aware that this must be incredibly difficult for him. Did he know about Allister? He continued,

'But something terrible has come to our attention. The Queen has managed to do that which we dread the most. She has infiltrated our ranks. A traitor is amongst us.'

There was a shuffling amongst the ranks and gasps and sighs could be heard across the room. The air was thick with tension.

'We have no other choice than to use the Heart Serum. Each of you is to line up row by row. You will come up to us here on the stage and take the Serum. We are greatly saddened to have to take these precautions, but treachery leaves us with no other option.' Taking a breath, Mr Sann continued,

'Row one, please lay down your swords and shields and meet us up here now.'

Two servants appeared out of nowhere and began to gather the swords and shields into large piles. It was clear that the soldiers felt uneasy about having their weapons removed from them. Line by line they moved onto the stage, like sheep being led to the slaughter. When they stood before Mr Sann each one was given a drop of the Heart Serum. Soldier after soldier was tested and each time light shone in his or her eyes. The relief was shared both by the soldier in question and by Mr Sann himself. I noticed that he kept glancing sideways, obviously looking out for his son. The knot in my stomach tightened as I realised that soon all rows of soldiers had been tested and still Allister had not appeared.

Had we been wrong to let him go? He couldn't possibly be a traitor, could he? I looked up at Gentle but his calm demeanour stilled my fears. He seemed to have an unyielding faith in Allister and no circumstances, no matter how terrible, phased him.

I longed to see Allister's face again, if only for a moment. I missed his deep blue eyes, his kind smile and his voice that could command an army just as easily as it could comfort a child. It terrified me to think that I might never see him again. Why had it taken such a terrible situation as this to make me realise how I felt about him? Would I ever be given a chance to tell him how I really felt? What if he did not feel the same?

I was snapped out of my thoughts by the sound of the trumpet blowing again. Every soldier had been tested. Something was wrong. Why hadn't Allister arrived and why had no traitor been found? The weapons were returned to the soldiers and it was obvious that they were relieved to be reunited with something that was so much a part of themselves. I glanced over at Gentle again, and now even he had a trace of anxiety on his face.

Mr Sann looked relieved that the test had shown that no soldier was a traitor, yet it was obvious that he was disturbed by his son's absence. One of the leaders next to him asked,

'Where is Allister?'

'I am not sure,' was Mr Sann's honest reply. 'But I know my son and he must have a reasonable explanation as to his absence at this time. It is not like him, as you all know. He is one of our most loyal and dedicated servants.'

'When will he take the Heart Serum?' someone shouted from the crowd.

Mr Sann's voice trembled as he answered,

'Allister took the test yesterday in front of us leaders and he passed as expected.'

'But how can we be sure? We need to see it,' another soldier cried out.

I gasped as a wave of discontentment swept through the room. The idea of a traitor had shaken the foundations of trust on which the Cave was based.

'My son will be here soon. Please trust him and remember all that he has done for you.' Mr Sann pleaded.

Mr Sann walked over to Gentle and me and asked,

'Do you two know anything as to Allister's whereabouts? This is just not like him. Something is wrong, I know it. Where is my son?' he asked in a commanding tone.

I dared not say anything and turned to Gentle, pleading him with my eyes to speak for us. Gentle breathed in heavily and spoke in a whisper,

'Mr Sann, I need you to trust. To trust me and your son. Right now I cannot tell you all the details but I do know that all is not as it seems. We have been infiltrated. Your son has been set up. I don't have all the answers yet, but give me some more time and we will find him and unravel this mess.'

Mr Sann was perplexed, he seemed to guess what had happened. He didn't ask any more questions but looked Gentle straight in the eye.

'You know that a great part of the destiny of the valley lies in Allister's hands. Without him, how will Abisha complete all she needs to learn?'

'Abisha!' he cried out suddenly, as if realising something for the first time. 'We must get her back into the Glass Room before anything else happens.'

Then, without so much as a word of explanation, I was rushed away, back to this room where I'm all alone again, with you dear Diary as my only companion.

Day 51

Dear Diary,

Who could have ever imagined all that I would share with you those weeks ago when I first brought you. If I had known what lay ahead of me, who's to say what I would have done.

Gentle visited me last night after the evening meal and spoke with me. He had met with Mr Sann and explained to him what had taken place. He knew Mr Sann would believe him as he had watched his son take the Heart Serum and pass it only hours before. Gentle relayed the conversation that had taken place between them. Mr Sann had said,

'We must keep this quiet from the other leaders. There is one, in particular, who has shown signs of jealousy towards Allister recently.' Mr Sann suspected that he could be involved in some way, but could not prove anything as he too had also passed the Heart Serum test.

'I will test him, Gentle. Stay clear and make sure Abisha is protected at all times. We know the traitor would want to get to her,' Mr Sann had warned. That is why they've placed me in the Glass Room. He encouraged me to read the books while I'm waiting for the next step.

'I'm scared, Gentle, and feel so alone.' I confessed.

'I know, child. It is a time of shaking amongst us. It is important to remember the foundation we stand upon which cannot be moved. It is just what the Queen wants, to bring division and mistrust amongst us at a time when we are about to expose and overthrow her kingdom. We must return to what we know and stand firm on that, with all we have. Read *The Heart of the Father*. Your father's words will reveal much of what Allister is not here to share.'

Once I was alone again I started reading the book. One passage in particular stunned me,

> What few of us understand is that the Mirror is a recent addition to the world we live in. This system, which controls all that we think and see in the valley, has not always existed. There was a time when laughter and freedom resounded from the valley. All were free to follow their dreams, to dress as they wanted, cut their hair as they liked. Each individual was beautiful in his or her own right. Comparison was something we did not have. The girls knew who they were and lived at peace with themselves and each other.

The words *the girls knew who they were* are still ringing in my head. Had I ever really known who I am? So much of my life have been plagued by self-doubt, fear and in the past few years even turned into more sinister and destructive self-hate and rejection. I'm beginning to discover who I am and to embrace this body and face of mine. I long to free the Reachables and my friends back at home from the Queen's grip. It is heart-breaking to know that they are still trapped. I had hoped we would return to help them soon but now, with Allister missing, who knows when we can make our move.

Allister, I find myself thinking about him constantly. What scares me more than never seeing him again is him returning and not feeling the same about me as I do for him.

Day 52

We still haven't heard anything from Allister and Gentle told me that rumours are spreading through the Cave that Allister is the traitor. It's unbearable to think that could be true and I'm desperate for him to reappear. I worry about him and hope that he's all right. I feel trapped in this Glass Room and this morning I woke up with a strong desire to visit the children. I called for Gentle and begged him to let me out, even for an hour. After checking with Mr Sann, they allowed me to visit the children's room after lunch. The purity of the children's hearts protects them from treachery, so being with them is safe for me. Gentle guarded me as I walked there and he took me through a secret corridor to prevent us from meeting anyone on the way.

It was wonderful to be with the children again. The awful tension that can be felt in the rest of the Cave wasn't present in their room. I was amazed at how welcome and at ease I felt amongst these young children. I wondered if they had ever struggled with the fear and the self-hate that I've battled with? Something tells me that they wouldn't even know what these things were.

They were playing when I arrived and I was surprised when Gentle called one girl to come over and talk to me. I thought she looked familiar as she came closer. She started to talk to me as if she knew what I was thinking.

'Hi, Abisha. Don't be afraid. Allister is the best and none of us are worried about him being a spy. We are sure that we can trust him. We just know it inside of us. He will be back soon. I know because …' At this point she moved closer to me and whispered into my ear, 'I know because we are in contact and he told me to tell you that he's safe. There's nothing to be afraid of. Oh, yes, he also said not to trust any leader except Mr Sann right now. He is very close to finding the true traitor. But he must stay hidden as long as his eyes are darkened.'

I was shocked and also relieved. Allister was safe and he thought to contact me. I felt instantly at home with the girl and answered her,

'Thank you for telling me these things, do you think you can get a message back to Allister for me?' I tried to sound relaxed and didn't want to let on how desperately I wanted to contact him or how much I missed him.

'Of course I can, he told me you would probably ask,' came her confident reply.

'Uh, oh, great. Then tell him, uh …' I was lost for words at this point and did not know how to continue.

'Tell him I'm okay and that I'm worried for him. Tell him that I miss him and hope he will be back soon. Tell him that I've started reading my father's book.' I didn't say more than that, I didn't dare to and I felt embarrassed.

'I'll pass on the message for you. Are you sure that there isn't anything else you want to say?' Her eyes sparkled as if she knew my true feelings for him.

'No, nothing else, thank you,' I stuttered.

I decided to turn my focus back to the girl and to find out some more information.

'What's your name? And how do you know so much about Allister?

'My name is Mary and Allister has been my teacher for many years. Actually,' she lowered her voice as she added, 'he's my brother.'

'Your brother!' I exclaimed. 'I didn't know that he had a sister.'

'Yes, he's my big brother. We have grown up together, here in the Cave, and Mr Sann is our daddy. Allister knows he can trust me and the other children and that's why he sent us a message. We are not afraid, Abisha, everything is going to work out fine. We just keep on singing our songs. That's what we have been taught to do. My daddy is strong and Allister is smart. They've got this worked out and I know they will do everything they can to protect me and the other children. They love me and I love them.'

How her words hit me hard. The strength in her childlike innocence was staggering and I felt as if there was enough power inside of her to change a city. I questioned why she had not been chosen to lead the army. It wasn't hard to believe that she was Allister's sister as I recognised so much of his kindness and courage in her.

'What do you think has happened to Allister?' I asked desperately. 'Does your father know anything?'

'Allister has been set up, that's all I know. I don't get it but I'm not worried. My brother is strong and he's clever. He will find whoever is to blame. Relax, Abisha. Believe in him and what he's told you. My big brother always comes through when you need him. He's the best.'

There was an insistency in her words and I knew that it was crucial that I listen to her. The whole situation has caused doubt to enter into my heart and affected my boldness.

'It's snack time now, I've got to go,' Mary said, 'but I promise to give him your message.'

And with that she threw her arms around me and gave me the warmest hug I've ever felt. She held on to me and her pure love and innocent trust poured into me. I felt like laughing and singing and all I could think was, *everything is going to be okay.* Hanging out with the children and especially Mary has that effect on you.

Day 53

My father's book astounds me. This morning I read about the power of the weak. In chapter four of his book he writes,

> There is a treasure in this world that many of us have yet to discover, the beauty of brokenness. Whenever you feel at your weakest and that there is nowhere else to turn, when you have lost all your own strength and no longer trust yourself – then you are ready to be trusted with power. Within the vulnerability of weakness where you have been stripped of your own ability, lies the power to change. When you no longer want to influence people for your own good, then and only then can true power be entrusted you.

As I read these words power charged through my veins. These were not simply words on a page, but seemed to have a life of their own, as if my father lived on through them. I continued to read the next chapter, this time on beauty. My father writes,

> True beauty lies not in the appearance but in the overflow of the heart. It is when we know that we are truly loved, when we are secure, that beauty permeates all that we say and do. We become a reflection of the treasure within us. It is then that true beauty shines through.

> Then we are not motivated by control, by placing ourselves above others because of our position. We have no need to dominate and oppress when we know who we are. True beauty breeds trust, trust

openness and openness, freedom. It is this inner freedom of the heart that we must offer the world.

My father seemed to be an amazingly wise man and his words paint a reality that seems so far removed from the world I grew up in.

After lunch I was told that I must continue with my training. I was thankful that I've been doing my push-ups every morning just as Allister told me to. He said that in order to master the sword I needed strength in my arms, and that muscles are only built through resistance. Gentle brought my weapons to the Glass Room in order for me to practise, as I'm still not allowed out. I trained and fought for hours. I missed the reassuring comments that Allister would normally give me, even those irritating ones that pushed me on when I wanted to give up. Gentle was there all the time and cheered me on as much as he could. I noticed that he was also affected by Allister's absence. His shoulders hung drooped and his eyes were blank.

'What's the purpose of my sword?' I asked, hoping to snap Gentle out of his sad state.

'Your sword is a crucial weapon. The more you become acquainted with it and understand how it works, the greater your ability to control it will be. Your sword is what will smash the works of the Queen. Your shield will always protect you, but the sword will both defend you and enable you to attack,' he answered, his face lighting up as he spoke.

'The sword epitomises all the truths that you've learnt and as it becomes one with your thoughts, you can use it to penetrate all that is false. Unless you believe in its power, it remains ineffectual. Your heart and your mind must become one with the sword and then in unison you can swing it.'

'Why must I practise for so long to understand this sword?' I wondered.

'Training is everything, Abisha. So many young recruits think that as soon as they have a sword in their hand they can use it, but that's only foolishness. A sword brings life and death and if used unwisely it can cause more damage than good. That's why you must learn to master it.'

'Who is it that we will use the sword against?' I asked anxiously. 'I would never want to hurt anyone, let alone kill them.'

'Our goal is not to kill, there is enough death and destruction in the valley as it is. The sword is to be used against the Mirror, and the mindset that has penetrated the valley. The sword will destroy all of the lies and cause them to evaporate. It's the mirrors, a false reflection of truth, that we are to aim for first. As we destroy them, the power of the Queen will radically diminish. She controls people through these mirrors. Her message is reinforced every time someone looks into them. That's why you had to learn to look into them and not be overcome by the messages they bring. You have done well to come this far and so quickly. The mark of your father is evident on your life and the quicker that you allow your mindset to be changed, the faster you will be able to overcome.'

'Why did you have to wait for me to be freed? Surely it would have been enough to enter the valley without me? What is it that I can bring that no one else can? I just don't understand. I feel so small and insignificant and in this place you've all learnt to follow the truth far longer than I have. Surely you are better equipped than I could ever be?'

I asked a lot of questions, but I really needed to understand. Ever since they had rescued me from the valley, I had been struggling with this question. Why me of all people? What could I do to help?

It was obvious that Gentle struggled to find the right words. Instinctively, I knew that he had the answers but was unable to tell me at this time.

'You will understand everything in good time. For now all that you need to know is that you are chosen. It is one thing to be called, but even the Chosen One must be made ready through instruction and discipline. You cannot overcome by mere will, you must allow yourself to grow and develop.'

I decided to leave it at that today and resolved to work harder on my sword lunges. If you only knew how much my arms ache after today's training. It is terrible. I could hardly lift them to dry myself after my much needed shower tonight. I still long for Allister.

Day 54

Mr Sann came to visit me this morning. His eyes were bloodshot with dark circles beneath them. He yawned as he walked in and he had clearly not been sleeping. He asked me how I was and how my training was going. I told him that I was learning a lot and felt more ready than ever. I also told him that I had been reading the history book he gave me, as well as my father's, *The Heart of the Father*. This seemed to please him and bring him some relief.

'There's not much time left and we have yet to discover who the real traitor is. Has anyone tried to contact you here?' he asked anxiously.

'No,' I replied. 'The only people I've spoken with are Gentle and your daughter, Mary.'

He didn't appear to be shocked, neither that I knew he had a daughter, nor that she had contacted me.

'Good,' was his only reply. 'That is as it should be.'

'We are close now, Abisha, to uncovering the traitor. There is to be a gathering of the leaders this afternoon. We want you to be there. As you look into the eyes of each one, the culprit will be exposed,' he stated mysteriously.

'What do you mean,' I wondered. 'Why do you need my help? Surely you don't mean that I can do anything? You have the Heart Serum for that.'

'We need you, Abisha. You hold a key,' he replied. 'Somehow the traitor has been able to tamper with the Heart Serum, but looking into the eyes will disclose everything.' He continued,

'It's not about what you can do, but about who you are. You are your father's child and nothing can change that or take it away from you. His heritage lies within you and it will shine out of you.'

I don't understand what he means but if me being present can help Allister and the People of the Cave, I am more than willing to help.

Evening

Mr Sann came to fetch me after lunch and he had a look of focus and resolve in his eyes that had been missing earlier this morning.

'I need you to trust me and to follow my instructions carefully,' were his first words to me. 'When I tell you to, you are to go past each leader that we have lined up and look them straight in the eye. We need you to wait at least five seconds by each one and if nothing happens, you are free to pass on to the next one,' he added.

'What kind of reaction are we looking for?' I wondered.

'It will be very clear. Your job is to look, mine will be to identify and apprehend the culprit. What we are looking for is a flash. You will see a flash of darkness and then the person will try to look away. You must hold their gaze for the full five seconds. Now come, it is time for us to go.'

I felt nervous as he led me to the strategy room. We walked into the room and I saw ten leaders in total lined up in a straight line. I recognised a few of them from my first days in the Cave. Amongst them was Mr Less who was a mentor to Mr Sann and had been part of the Cave since the early days. I knew that he meant a great deal to Mr Sann and that he, especially after my father's disappearance, had been an enormous source of comfort and wisdom. There were two brothers who had also been around from the beginning. I also recognised a lady called Ebba who was in charge of teaching the children. I had liked her straight away and was particularly drawn to her kindness. I felt safe around her and desperately hoped that she would not be involved in any way. The others, I didn't know by name. They were lined up one after another and none of them seemed to know what was about to happen.

Mr Sann motioned me to start walking and I began. The first person was one of the brothers and I looked him straight in the eye. Under my breath I counted slowly,

'One, two, three, four ...'

When I came to five, to my relief, nothing happened. I moved on to his brother next to him. Nothing happened there either. Now it was Ebba's turn. She looked back at me, unmoved. I started to count and felt that she would have been able to hold my gaze for hours,

'... four, five.'

Ebba's eyes shone and I felt strengthened by our contact. I knew that when I was let out of the Glass Room, she was someone I wanted to spend more time with and that, on the battlefield, she would be an invaluable resource and friend. I sighed a breath of relief and steadied myself as I reached the next one.

I went through seven of them and none reacted with any flash of darkness. I looked beside me and saw that Mr Less was next to be tested. I was pleased that it was his turn, confident that such a faithful father could never be known as a traitor. I turned to face him and he flinched. He looked me straight in the eye and I was sure this would be over quickly. I counted as I had with the others:

'One, two, three, four,' no change and then, 'five'. Suddenly the whole room began to swirl and what happened next was a blur. Just as I counted five his eyes changed colour and a dreadful darkness filled their core and a black flash reflected from them. Then he cried out,

'Stupid girl, why did we have to bring her to the Cave? She has ruined everything now. If only we had left her there to starve herself to death. I could have helped you all. Don't you know all I have done to serve and help you? You would think that was enough for you. But no, you all chose to go after this little girl. What can she bring? You may think that I'm the traitor, but actually she is. If she had remained in the valley none of this need have happened. If only you had all seen that I'm the one that is meant to help you and not her, then all would have been as it should be.' The intensity of the hate behind his words was awful and I struggled to breathe after his outburst.

Mr Sann reacted quickly, grabbing hold of this older man that he clearly loved and respected. 'Take him to the room and treat him gently.'

Immediately three armed soldiers took hold of him by the arms and, with dignity and respect, carried him away. Gentle ran over to me and threw his arms around me. I was sobbing and shaking.

'I don't understand,' I cried out. 'Was this all my fault? Why was he so angry with me? What will happen to him now? Where is Allister?'

'Don't accuse yourself, Abisha. This is not your fault. This is about a man who allowed ambition and deceit to enter into his heart. Mr Less had great influence and was trusted here in the Cave. His role was to serve and protect the Servants of the Court, but clearly pride crept in and destroyed everything for him. Your arrival exposed what was hiding in his heart and he must have set Allister up in order to remove him and to hinder you from completing your task. He must have been tempted to go over to the ways of the Mirror and the Queen. Mr Sann will handle this for now. Let us get you back to the room, it is probably safest to keep you theres until we have fully grasped the entirety of the situation.'

He came to check on me later and informed me of the latest news that the Queen has been gathering her troops again. Reports from the valley are that the restrictions of the Mirror have stepped up dramatically. Fear is rampant and Agents of the Mirror regularly patrol through the streets of Genville. There are even reports that a fresh shipment of mirrors have been brought in and that orders have gone out requiring that all inhabitants spend at least two hours every day looking into them. Those mirrors! How it angers me to think that my friends must be forced to look into them even longer.

I just wish that Allister was here right now so that I could talk to him about all that I have on my heart. But at least the traitor has been exposed.

Day 55

Mr Less has been detained and peace has returned to the Cave. Now we are waiting for Allister to return.

Mr Sann came to talk to me this morning. He was sad but also relieved that the traitor had been exposed. I know that Mr Less had meant so much to him in the past and this was a painful blow for him, too. Like Gentle, he assured me that what had happened was not my responsibility and encouraged me by saying I had been very brave. Before I could even ask he said,

'We still don't know where Allister is. We expect that he will appear at any time, now that Mr Less has been exposed. The Queen is moving in and we must be sure of how much Mr Less has shared with her. It seems that he had agreed to betray Allister in order to hinder your training and to hurt us as a family.'

There was anguish in his voice as he spoke. For a moment, I was able to look past my own pain and focus on what must be going on in the heart of this man. The fresh lines on his brow and tightness around his mouth disclosed the tension and battle he had undergone. He looked older today. His face spoke of both the grief and betrayal he had suffered and of his determination and steadfast loyalty to the cause. I knew the depth of character and love he carried came at a great price.

'What do you want me to do?' I asked, desperate to help in any way I could.

'I want you to stay here and finish reading your father's book. It is vital that you know the whole truth before I send you out into the battle. Remain here, read, gain strength and understanding. When Allister returns we will be ready to move forward again. You should know that your father would be so proud of you. You are a brave one and I am confident that you will lead the army well. You have the heart of a lion, and you will lead us into victory, of that I'm sure.'

His words were both comforting and disturbing. I knew he wouldn't speak unless he meant it. That much I understood about him and still I doubted my own ability to succeed, let alone lead an army. Me, brave? So many times I had felt like such a failure and coward and could hardly see how anyone, especially my father, could be proud of me right now. I thanked him for his words and determined to finish the book as soon as possible.

I've been reading all afternoon. It's strange to read his words, as if he was aware of the struggle I had had – me and so many others back in the valley. He writes,

A key expression of loving oneself is to give our bodies that which we need in order to survive. Food is a gift but the Queen has taken it and turned it into a weapon. A weapon of destruction which she uses to control and manipulate people. She has started a new trend where young people are being taught to punish themselves through starvation.

We must fight this trend with all our efforts. Should these young people be denied the very thing they need? It is the Queen's strategy to convince these precious ones that they are enhancing and empowering themselves by rejecting food in this way. The fear and threat of becoming fat has infiltrated the valley to such an extent that our own children are being sacrificed because of it. To be taught that the way they are is not acceptable and that they must change. They try everything to become something that they already are. Beautiful and accepted. This is a great tragedy and must be fought with all our strength.

We must not allow the message of the Queen, through her mirrors, to reach their tender hearts or our world will dissolve. The very ones who are our future will be destroyed. They will never become who they are meant to be. Her lies will rob them of their strength and destiny and our world will be denied their gift. We cannot let the Queen and her Mirror infiltrate the minds of these young ones anymore. We must act but we must do it quickly. Time is running out in the valley. Who will fight for these ones?

Who will fight for these ones? His question haunts me. Could it possibly be that I'm able to help others from something that I myself have been so bound?

His words captivate me. I know they are true and yet I'm painfully aware of how deeply I've fallen into the very trap he described, to long to have the body that the Reachables presented and, most of all, be driven by the fear of becoming fat.

He makes everything seem so simple and clear. But, I know first hand that being caught up in this world is often brutal, confusing and deceptive. It is truly a battlefield and easy to be taken captive.

But it is time to fight back. Just as I've been set free, so thousands of others can be.

Day 56

I woke to the sound of singing today. It was the sound of the children's song. I jumped out of bed and followed the voices until I found them gathered in their classroom. Each child was singing, a symphony of new sounds and lyrics and together they were creating a beautiful new song. I felt like I could listen forever. For every line they sang, fresh hope filled me. These young children truly possess a strength that is phenomenal.

Their teacher, Ebba, was there, conducting them as they sang. She managed to instil a sense of security among them, whilst in no way hindering them from expressing themselves freely. I could only dream of flowing with them like this one day. I listened to the words they were singing,

There is a sound of freedom in our veins,
We are the generation of hope,
We are the children of light.
Truth is what we fight for, hope is the gift we bring.

We choose the way of life,
We choose to make our voices known.
We come with open hands,
We will not force ourselves in.

Will you hear the sound of our singing?
Will you open your hearts to our song?
Our gift is yours to receive.
Truth is what we fight for, hope is the gift we bring.

These were a generation of children so different from those in the valley. They could bring about change armed with weapons of love, innocence and courage. How I wish that I had what they possess.

I let the sound of their song fill me and the longer I listened, the larger hope grew inside of me. I was struck by how different these children were compared to the servants of the Queen. They have nothing to prove, unabsorbed with how they look. They radiate and are the face of true beauty. As soon as they had finished singing, I walked over to Mary,

'That's a beautiful song, Mary,' I said. 'It really touched my heart and filled me with hope. Where did you learn such sounds?'

'These are our freedom songs, Abisha,' she answered. 'We have sung them all our lives. It's all we know.'

'Is it possible to learn these songs for people like me who haven't grown up here?' I wondered, almost afraid to hear her answer.

'Of course,' she replied. 'The songs of freedom can be learnt by anyone. It just takes a longer time for people who haven't grown up in the Cave like us. You will have to remove the songs from the valley that have filled your heart. Only once they've been removed can you begin to learn our songs.'

I was shocked at her reply. Songs in the valley? I had no memory of hearing any.

'What do you mean? We never learnt to sing in the valley. I don't understand.'

'There are songs and sounds all around us,' she replied. 'Messages that fill the atmosphere. The sounds that you learnt in the valley, you never recognised as a song but it was one that the Mirror plays across the valley day and night. It's a hidden message that seeps into your mind until you no longer question it. Neither the Mirror, nor the Queen want you to realise that it's being sung at all. That's why is it so effective and destructive.'

'But, what does the song sound like?' I wondered. 'I ve never heard it before.'

'What did you feel when you looked into the mirrors in the valley?' Mary asked.

I thought back to all those times when I had looked into the mirrors and suddenly the fragmented feelings I had felt joined together into a terrible song.

We are singing you a song your conscious cannot hear.
Look into our mirrors, we will show you truth
Dream not of being loved. Stay trapped in fear.
Things will stay the same, you will never change.

You are ugly, you are fat. Your appearance is a disgrace.
Learn to hate yourself, deny yourself all joy.
You will never be a Reachable. You have no place.
No hope, no hope, we offer you no hope.

I was astounded. Could it really be that this song had been sung over me in the valley all these years and that I had never realised it? It was a horrible thought and I struggled to take it in.

'Have you heard anything from Allister?' I asked, changing the subject.

'No, I haven't,' she replied. 'He hasn't come to me again. But I'm sure he's safe and will come back to us soon.'

'Ok, just please let me know when you hear from him,' I begged.

'Of course I will. Now it's time for us to sing again,' she replied.

I left these precious children who despite being so young have so much wisdom. After talking to Mary I decided to finish the last chapter of my father's book. Interestingly enough the final chapter was titled, 'Freedom – The Inheritance of All'. My father writes,

Freedom is the journey that every person finds themselves on. We long to know that we are loved and accepted for who we are and not for what we do. This is even more vital when talking about our core being. Each child must be taught their inherent worth. We must train the future generations and encourage them always. They will be taught to sing songs of hope. Songs that fill the atmosphere and bring new life. We must protect them form the voice of doubt, the voice of self-hate. The Queen and her Mirror are planning an attack on the core of our young ones. We must uncover this strategy and protect them. They will not know that they are caught up in it. Once entangled, only the voice of truth will set them free. Let the sounds of freedom be released in the valley, we must learn to sing them daily and teach those younger than us to dream. They hold the key to freedom.

It was then that I read these shocking words,

Now I will become personal in my writing. I have a daughter who is still very young. She is my greatest joy and I love her more than my own self. She is one of these who will bring a message of hope. She is a forerunner of the new generation. My daughter and others like her will accomplish what we may have failed to do. May she be protected always and those like her.

It felt unreal to read about myself and to believe that my own father had written these words long before I was ever able to understand them. I felt close to him, somehow connected through his words. I wondered if he had known that I would read this one day? If only I had been able to meet him and talk to him. But he's gone from my life and now Allister seems to be, too. I know I must be brave and trust, but I feel so alone without them.

At least Gentle came to visit me after my evening meal. He sat in the armchair opposite my bed and we didn't say much to each other. We didn't need to. I knew he shared my sorrow over Allister's disappearance and I knew that he cared. Gentle's task is to protect me and I don't doubt that he even would be willing to die for me.

This strong, battle-worn soldier. He must have seen so much in his lifetime and still he has a humility and kindness about him that is rare. These are character traits that are looked down upon in the valley, caring for another was seen as the ultimate form of weakness. I'm so thankful for Gentle and I need him desperately.

I decided to ask him more about my Father,

'What was my father like, Gentle?' I asked.

'Come and sit closer, dear child,' Gentle beckoned and I sat by his feet, hungry for every word he had to say.

'Your father was a man like no other. When he walked through the Cave he carried such respect with him that everyone would bow as he passed by. He never demanded this respect though and would become shy and embarrassed at the honour shown him. No, he was not one to demand, but he won the love and hearts of everyone in this place. There wasn't one in his army who wouldn't have been willing to lay down his life for him and for the cause.

Your father lived not for himself or his own glory but always for the good of others. He was known to stop and pick up rubbish he passed on his way. Refusing to allow another to do it for him. He believed that it is in the small, insignificant and menial tasks of life that true character is revealed. He didn't seem to differentiate between leading an army into battle, or cleaning the bathrooms. All were equally important to him. The importance was not the task but the manner in which it was done. Even a tyrant can do great acts of bravery, but only a leader with a servant's heart is willing to lay down his life for others.

His way of treating others was also exceptional. He never differentiated people's worth according to their rank or position and would show the same kindness and respect to everyone he met.

If there were any group where his heart was slightly partial, however, it was the children. He really loved them. Every morning he would check in on them. He would lift them up into his arms, hug them and speak words of life and hope to each one. There was never a day that he missed this morning routine. Even when he was burdened with the threat of attack, he would give these young ones his devotion and love. He never let them see the pain or trouble he was feeling and many times I wondered if they were not the source of his strength. He was a wonderful man, Abisha, and you remind me of him many times. It doesn't surprise me that you love to visit the children. You are your father's daughter.'

It was wonderful to hear these words about this man that I loved. Yet it also brought up great grief in my heart. The sorrow of not having him in my life is starting to catch up with me. I also wondered why I had not been with him in the Cave when I was a child. Why he had spent time with them and not with me? Gentle noticed my anguish and said,

'I imagine talking about your father must raise lots of questions in you. All will be revealed when the time is right. We must sleep now, dear one. Each day has its own battle and we do not know what tomorrow will bring. No matter your concerns, sleep peacefully in the knowledge that you are deeply loved.'

I guess all I can do now is trust.

Day 57

I awoke to the sounds of trumpets this morning. Their rich, commanding noise resounded through the air. There was an urgency and authority about it. Instinctively, I knew it was a call to gather and prepare. The sound of war is in the air.

I ate my breakfast with fervency, sensing that I would need all my strength today. I chose to visit the children as soon as I had finished. They seemed to be expecting me and ran towards to me. I picked each one up into my arms and whispered words of encouragement into their ears. I felt a charge of strength surge through me. I saw Gentle smiling at me from the doorway. His eyes sparkled and his grin said it all. He told me that Mr Sann wanted to see me and we went to meet him in the strategy room.

'How are you dear Abisha? Have you finished reading *The Heart of the Father* now?' he asked.

'I'm fine, sir, and yes, I finished the book yesterday. I'm lost for words. I understand so little, but I know that I'm called,' was all I could utter.

'Do not worry, Abisha. Freedom and truth will speak for themselves. They live on through your father's words and now that you have read them they will forever be a part of you. But now to the business of the day,' he added with a serious tone.

'It is time to act. Today we will prepare. Tomorrow we must go to war. You are to address the troops this afternoon and we will commence our attack tomorrow morning. We have reports that the Queen is gathering her troops. We have our orders and cannot wait any longer. Mr Less' treachery has forced us to speed up our attack. We just cannot afford to wait any longer.'

'But what about Allister,' I cried out. 'Surely we cannot go into battle without him? Where is he? How can I fight without him?'

'I understand your concern, Abisha,' he answered. 'We all feel his absence acutely. We still do not know where he is and he hasn't been in contact with Mary again. As his father I ache for him, but as the commander of these armies I must now choose what is best for the valley and for our soldiers. I know my son, even if it means sacrificing himself he will do it, to save the valley and ...' he hesitated, 'to protect you.'

My body shook as he spoke and I dared not even think the worst. I wanted to scream, *No! Please don't make me do this alone, please don't tell me that I may never see Allister again.*

'None of us want to be in this without him and yet here we are left with no choice but to move on.'

'I'm willing to do what I must,' I answered as bravely as I could. The quiver in my voice still giving me away. 'I will prepare myself to address the troops. I need my armour and I need some time alone to think and prepare.'

'Of course, take all the time you need. We will gather after midday in the Assembly Hall,' Mr Sann said.

'Thank you, Abisha,' he added. 'Thank you for sacrificing yourself for us. I know this must be hard for you. Take comfort. You are stronger than you think Don't look to or rely on your own abilities but depend on the fact that you are chosen. The seeds of destiny were planted inside of you and they've been watered and nourished. The seeds have now grown into a beautiful plant and it is time for you to bloom. We stand with you, Abisha, and even without Allister you can do this. Surrender to the call and let it empower you.'

He reached over and placed something into the palm of my hand.

'Your father gave me this to give you many years ago. He knew that this day would come and he prepared for it in great detail. I think he sensed that somehow he might not be able to be here in person. He gave me this package and told me to give it to you. I've kept it safe all this time and now it is yours to open.'

I looked at the small package in my hands and was overcome by a desire to open it immediately.

'Take it back with you to the Glass Room and open it there,' directed Mr Sann, as if he understood the urgency I felt. 'It is important that you are alone and that you have time to absorb the contents.'

'Thank you, Mr Sann,' I stuttered, 'I'll see you in the Assembly Hall at 2 o'clock.'

I ran all the way back to the Glass Room and stood looking at the package, terrified and intrigued. At last my curiosity overtook my fear and I tore open the package. At first I only saw a letter. The faded colour of the paper and musty smell disclosed that it must have been written years ago. Then as I opened the letter a small, golden pocket mirror appeared. At first I found this strange. A mirror was the last thing I thought that my father would want me to have, especially after all the trouble and anguish they had caused me up to this point. I carefully placed the mirror to the side and decided to read the letter first.

My beloved Abisha,

If you are reading this letter right now then I know that my worst fears have been confirmed, that I am not there to support you in this difficult time. Please know that I hoped it would never come to this but, as you now understand, the strategies of the Queen and the Mirror are devious and effective.

Before I write anything else, I want you to know that my love for you is unending. Death itself, though it separates us for a time, cannot keep us apart forever. You are mine, my beloved daughter. Know that your birth was the most joyous day of my life and that I so longed for you to grow up knowing me. There is much that you have had to learn on your own. That saddens me. I always wanted to be there encouraging, coaching and loving you each step of the way. I am sorry that I was not able to.

By this point you must have realised that you have been called to a great task and now is the time when you must embrace your destiny. I trust that you have been well prepared and that there are those around you who support and protect you. There is a boy who was born just four days earlier than you who I sense will be a great help for you. His name is Allister and he is the son of my dear friend. If you have not already met him, find him, he holds a key for you.

I imagine that you might be terribly afraid right now but I tell you don't fear, my dear one. Every great warrior has had to meet their fears on the edge of the battlefield. You are no exception. Don't bow down to fear, but rather, let your love for the people in the valley override it. Love is your most powerful weapon. Not a weak, sentimental love, but one that dares to speak the truth and stand up for what is right, even in the midst of great opposition.

You will not be overcome. This is your hour. You will lead the army and be greater than I ever was. If I was there right now I would take you into my arms, hold you and whisper all the love and encouragement you need into your ears. But because you are reading this letter all you have are my words.

I have left a gift for you. Open it and look into it. I know you may wonder why a mirror? Trust me. Look into it and take it with you onto the battlefield.

Remember who you are, Abisha. Use the authority you have been given to set others free. Do not abuse it, or use it to dominate others. Instead, become the servant of all and let humility be your ally. Take courage, my daughter.

With all my love which reaches beyond the grave,
Your father

Tears streamed down my face as I read his words. To think that he had written to me all those years ago and prepared me for this day. If only I could have him here with me right now.

'Father, father! Where are you?' I cried out. 'Father, I need you so desperately right now.'

My cries echoed hauntingly around the room and I could do nothing but accept the fact that he is not here with me and never can be.

I turned towards the mirror and studied it. It was simple but had a striking beauty about it. There was a golden rim around the oval shaped mirror. It was different from the rectangular shaped mirrors I knew from the valley. It intrigued me. I found it confusing that my father, on the most important day of my life, would give me one. I chose to trust him despite my own reservations and opened up the cover to look into it.

At first there was nothing special about it, all I saw was my questioning face staring back at me. But then, oh Diary, I wish you were able to see what I saw at that moment. I saw my father's face. He was alive, looking back at me and smiling. His eyes sparkled and despite the seriousness of the moment he was full of joy.

I turned away for a moment and then looked back at it again to make sure that I wasn't imagining the whole thing. But as soon as I glanced again, his face appeared before me.

I noticed that his lips were moving and he was saying something to me. I couldn't hear the words, I only saw his lips move. I strained my eyes to look closer and tried to read his lips. The more I looked into this enchanting mirror, the more I sensed my mind change. I knew my father was trying to communicate something to me, but for now all I could see was his reflection.

Eventually, I closed the mirror and took a few moments to let it all sink in. He's a part of me and I'm a part of him. He gave me two gifts today, his words and his reflection. They are enough for me to face the day ahead of me. My father's letter confirmed what my heart has come to know. Allister and I are connected and he holds a key for me.

Now I must prepare my speech for the troops.

Evening

I finished preparing my speech and Gentle came to fetch me. I stood at the door of the Assembly Hall and looked out over the army that was gathered. It was an intimidating scene, hundreds upon hundreds of soldiers clothed in their magnificent golden armour. They rose to greet me as I walked into the hall, and as they did, flashes of light and gold reflected throughout the room, from their swords. It was a breathtaking sight. I heard hushed tones as I walked onto the stage they had prepared for me. I looked out over the sea of expectant faces, looking to me to lead and inspire them and suddenly a wave of self-doubt washed over me.

Lead them? How can I do that? How can someone who has been so bound by fear, instil courage and faith into these mighty warriors? What could I possible say to these people to convince them, and myself, that I was worthy?

My thoughts plagued me and I began to regret agreeing to this whole thing. But then, as I reached the podium in front of the troops and turned to address them, the most wonderful thing happened. A surge of power flowed through me. I stood there, little me who only a few weeks earlier had wanted to die and without warning, suddenly I knew it. I was born for this – this is who I really am. I am a warrior, called to lead these forces to set others free from the confusion and deception of the Queen and her Mirror. At that moment I could almost feel my father beside me, breathing his encouragement on me.

I took a deep breath and turned to face the vast crowd of soldiers saying,

'Dear chosen ones, Servants of the Court, I am honoured to stand before you today. I am a girl, young and inexperienced. I know little of the battles that you have had to endure, or of the sacrifices that you have made for others and even for me. I know little of how to use the sword or the shield. What I have come to understand is that the blood of my father flows in my veins. I have only recently discovered that my father was a great man and deeply loved by you all. I am sad that I lost him so early and yet I sense that he is here with us now, in some form.

I have been chosen to lead you into battle. I cannot promise you that I will lead perfectly, I am still learning, but I will stand by your side. There are many like me out there in the valley: men, women and children who have been caught in the Queen's web of lies. There are those who struggle with their identity, striving to change their appearance by starving and wounding themselves and whom the Mirror has ordained will soon take their own lives. We have the power to help them and we must not back down from the task. This is our hour, and if you will accept me as your leader, I will do my best. Let us stand and cry out for the people of the valley.'

How I wish you had been there to hear the roar that rose from the army, it was as if the mountains themselves shook and the ground beneath us began to tremble.

'Freedom for the trapped ones!' was trumpeted through the air.

I was quite undone and hardly recognised the girl who stood there and had just given this speech. Gentle turned towards me and said,

'You are truly the one we have been waiting for. I hear the sound of your father in your voice. His light shines from within you. Trust that inheritance. It is there. Walk in it.'

Then Gentle, the guardian that I've come to love and trust, picked me up into his arms and squeezed me so hard that I thought all the air would be sucked right out of me.

Mr Sann said he had never seen the troops so ready for battle. Tomorrow we will leave for the valley and I don't know what awaits me there. Diary, if this is to be my last entry, please know that I've been so happy to have you to talk to. You have been a great strength to me and helped me to process the events of the past few weeks. You will come with me into the battle and I only hope that I live to write to you again.

Day 58

Today was a day like no other. After a good night's sleep and a hearty breakfast, we assembled outside the Cave, ready to descend into the valley. Spirits were high amongst the soldiers and there was a sense of devotion and respect within the ranks, like an army working together in total unity. Such a stark contrast to the fear and guilt which the Queen's kingdom is led by. My thoughts turned again towards the hundreds of girls who were under her control. If only we could get to them, I know that we could free them to be themselves.

The soldiers looked magnificent. Their golden armour glimmered in the morning sun and I was forced to look away for as the brightness of their reflection blinded me momentarily.

I had my full armour on, dressed in – as I now knew – my father's sword, shield and helmet. It was almost comical seeing myself dressed up like this with such a noble army behind me. Despite the seriousness of the moment I found myself letting out a giggle.

The sound of metal scraping against metal filled the air. The ground shook underneath the weight of the army as they ran on the spot. The atmosphere was charged. I took my place at the front and was ready to give the marching orders when, suddenly, I saw the children come forward out of the Cave. They walked past the soldiers in formation with a determination and clarity of purpose in their steps and came to a standstill by my side. This can't be, I thought, and looked around. Was anyone else going to react? We were about to go into battle, surely you don't put children on the front lines? I turned to Mr Sann and asked,

'Are you going to say something to the children? Shouldn't we move them away from the front?'

Mr Sann looked at me, patiently, before answering,

'Abisha, this army is like no other on this earth. We do not fight with the weapons that other armies do. We fight in an invisible realm. Apart from you, the children are our greatest weapon. It is the song from their pure hearts, resounding in the atmosphere, that protects us as we move forward towards the valley. The Queen and her forces hate the sound of freedom and their power weakens the more the children sing. We are allowing them to go in front of us because they have asked to have this place. In fact, they begged us to be positioned there. They are not afraid. They are true warriors and heroes. But do not fear for their lives, it is our responsibility and joy to protect them in all they do. We will not put them at any unnecessary risk.'

I was shocked by his reply. Nothing in the world of the Cave is as it is in the valley. In the valley children were not counted on for anything. I was reminded of Gentle's words about my father, how he had visited the children every day of his life. He must have understood the power that they carried.

I walked over to the children. They were glowing, each one dressed in beautiful golden garments (just like the one I had worn on my 18th birthday). They did not carry any swords or shields and their song seemed to be their only weapon. Their eyes shone like fire. These were children who understood more about their identity than any of the adults I had ever met in the valley. I still felt that they looked out of place on this battlefield. I turned to Mary who was staring at me intensely.

'We're with you Abisha,' she stated firmly. You don't need to be scared about today. We will sing until the last of the Queen's army has fallen. We are not afraid. We have been preparing ourselves for this moment our whole lives. You must lead, Abisha, with strength. We will prepare a way for you. Use your sword. Don't let it leave your side. Take up your banner and let it fly over your head.'

My banner, I had almost forgotten about my banner. I took it out of its protective cover and had it ready.

I thanked Mary and the children as they gathered around me and gave me a warm hug.

'We love you Abisha,' they cried out together.

I felt strength surge through me and the worry that had consumed me just moments before evaporated. I was about to return to my place when Mary whispered into my ear,

'Don't worry about Allister. He will come back. Wait and trust. He will appear when you need him the most.' I hoped that her words were true, I wished that he could be there with me.

Ebba motioned for the children to stand in line. I was relieved to see her there with them. I raised my banner and waved it in the air above me. As I did, a warm breeze blew over us.

I called out, 'Forward, march!'

We started to move towards the valley, the song of the children penetrated the air,

> *We are the chosen ones, we are the free.*
> *We will not back down to the forces that control.*
> *With fear and guilt we will not agree.*

We are the beautiful ones, precious and loved.
Just as we are, that is our key.
That is the way that we will lead.

Further and further down the valley we moved. We passed the halfway mark where the valley people would come to picnic. We entered the gate of Genville and passed the fountain. I listened for a moment as it bubbled and gurgled. It seemed almost unreal that we were to face some kind of confrontation on this day. We moved forward and I was overcome with memories of this place that had been my home. I felt radically different from the person I was when I was taken from the valley only weeks ago.

As I looked around, I was struck by how empty it was. The streets were barren. The shop doors closed. Where was everyone? What was going on in this place? Even for the valley where oppression and fear were familiar feelings, it was clear that something was wrong. Not even the Reachables were anywhere to be seen. They usually paraded these streets, like lions lurking by every street corner, looking for any bait that they could devour.

We walked past the bakery. There was no aroma of tempting donuts or freshly baked bread coming from it, just the musty smell of dust and debris. I saw an old loaf of bread on the floor beside the rubbish bin. I kicked at it and it was hard as a football. It must have been lying there for days.

Advancing past my old home, I looked up at the window on the sixth floor. I wondered if my aunt was inside. I shuddered to think that I had almost jumped out of that very window. How close I had been to ending everything. Little did I know then what lay ahead of me.

An eagle flew past me just as it had done all those weeks ago and in that moment I knew what needed to be done.

'Aim for the mirrors!' I cried out. 'We must destroy them all.'

We charged into town. I lifted up my sword, just as they had shown me, and struck it directly into the centre of the first mirror I found. At first there was resistance and it appeared as if the sword had no power. I continued to press it into the core of the mirror and then, just as they had promised me it would, it broke. Pieces of glass scattered everywhere and I heard a high-pitched scream as the mirror disintegrated into nothing. As soon as a glass piece touched the ground, it evaporated into thin air, as if it had never been there.

We moved swiftly through the middle of the street. I knew that at the end of it was the place to where the largest mirror was positioned. I don't know how I had not realised before that this was where the Mirror had its stronghold, but in that moment I knew it. I had always been afraid to walk past that one. It had a powerful magnetic pull, but even as a child something had told me that I must resist looking into it at all costs. Instinctively, I knew that if I looked inside of it, I would be destroyed. I was now drawn towards this place, knowing that I now came neither weak, nor defenceless.

I reached the front of the Mirror and was about to lift my sword towards it when, suddenly, the Queen appeared surrounded by her army of Reachables. I was shocked to see her there. Her face glared at me with ice-cold hate as did each one of her company of

Reachables. Dread washed over me and flashbacks of the trauma of trying out for the Reachable hit me, once again. What was happening, had she regained her power over me? Wasn't my sword strong enough to defeat her and the mirrors?

'Do you really think that you can defeat me, child?' she hissed. 'How dare you enter into my territory and destroy my mirrors? You will pay dearly for what you have done. There is no mercy in my kingdom. You know the punishment for turning against me. You should have considered that before you chose to enter into this battle.'

I panicked and I didn't know which way to turn. For a second, all my training was put on the line and I seemed unable to remember anything. I was paralysed and dared not look at her or the girls. She continued,

'Do you really think that you can come here and just change everything? The kingdom that I have created is not so easily destroyed. I have worked many years to perfect this valley and I am not going to let a young, insignificant, rebellious and above all *fat* girl destroy my life's work. Move aside child and go back to where you belong, in the shadows.'

Her words pierced my heart. The word that I so dreaded, fat, reverberated in my mind. I found myself being sucked into her message, despite all that I had learnt in the Cave. Memories of trying out for the Reachables, the words of the judges and the scorn of the other contestants flashed through my mind. The longer she stood before me, the harder it was to think clearly. I stood frozen. Why was I here again? What was my assignment? I let my sword hang beside my body and my banner began to drag on the ground. At the back of my mind, I vaguely remembered my shield and knew that I should be lifting it up right now. It seemed so heavy and hung on my arm more like a burden than a help.

'You see, you stupid child, you have no power over me. There is nothing you can do to stop me. Just give in now and accept your failure. You are nothing but a fat, foolish failure. Her face contorted at this point and the ageless beauty that she had when I first met her was gone. Her features twisted with malicious hate and she looked hideous. I shuddered as she kept on speaking,

'You should have stayed with me in my kingdom. If only you had let me take your mind. What a great team we could have been.'

As she spoke the word *team*, I looked up and suddenly I heard a familiar voice cry out from behind me.

'Abisha, take up your sword, remember your training! Lift up your head and raise your banner. Place the shield over your heart. Her words won't be able to penetrate you with the shield in place.'

My heart stopped beating. I knew that voice. Could it be?

'Allister!' I cried out. 'Is that you? Is it really you?' I turned around and saw him standing in front of me. I wanted to run straight into his arms.

'Are you all right, are you hurt?'

There was no time to hear his answer or to tell him all I wanted to say. I had just enough time to bring forward my shield before the Queen interrupted us,

'How very sickening to see the two of you together, the children of my enemies. You disgust me. Get out of my way.'

Her words had lost their power and threat now that Allister was standing beside me. I lifted my sword in one hand and my banner in the other and as I did a blinding light filled the valley. I stretched out my sword towards the Queen and spoke,

'You have no power over me anymore. I am a child of my father and the truth that the people the Cave have shown me has given me freedom. You speak nothing but lies, Queen. Pure fabrications! Your words do not define me. I am not a failure and I am certainly not fat. I am beautiful and I am chosen. Fat is a figment of your own mind. Today, I choose freedom. I will no longer listen to your lies and accusations. You have ruled this valley long enough.'

As I spoke the army behind me raised their swords in unison and fresh courage and resolve flowed through me.

'I declare a new day in this place. Let the ground cry out that the rule of the Mirror is no more. People are free to be themselves.'

The Queen's eyes turned black and the force of her seething anger created a vaporous fog around her. Allister placed his hand on mine and an electric current flowed through us. He grabbed hold of my sword and together we lifted it straight into the air. We cried out together, instinctively knowing what to say,

'We raise the sound of freedom over everything in this place. We don't come against you in our own power, Queen, but in the power of truth that our fathers have taught us. We will not accept your lies and we will not bow down to your threats.'

With those words, Allister whispered in my ear, 'Now walk towards her and face her.' He let go of my sword and indicated that this was something only I could do.

The Queen stood like a statue in front of me. I walked towards her with my sword held out in front of me. I moved closer and closer and yet she remained in my path. I looked back at Allister, seeking his advice.

'Just keep walking, Abisha. You can do it. Keep walking.'

I walked and began to realise that this would be a test of wills. The Queen refused to budge. I continued to move forward. I was only a few paces from her and had no other choice. I could not bow down to her now. I closed my eyes and lunged forward fully expecting my sword to pierce her belly, but I didn't hear her cry out. I walked right through her and felt nothing. She was no longer there and had evaporated into thin air. I wondered if I had imagined the whole thing. Where had she gone?

'Well done, Abisha!' I heard Allister cry out.

'Keep walking now and destroy the Mirror.'

I was shocked, but had no time to reflect on what had just happened. Walking up the steps that the Mirror was placed on, I reached the last step and took up my sword one last time. I lifted it high into the air and plunged it right into the centre of the Mirror, but nothing happened. Had I missed something, I wondered?

'Lay down your sword now. Use your banner. Wave it in front of the Mirror.'

As I took up my banner, relief washed over me. I had always felt more at ease and one with my banner than with my sword. I waved it back and forth, hesitantly at first and then more fervently. My mind did not fully understand, but my heart sensed that things were changing. The sound of singing filled the air and I knew the children were close by. My banner and their voices unified in the sound of freedom. I carried on waving it to the melody I heard.

The Mirror began to show cracks in its corners, small fissures at first that grew the more I waved. Then the small cracks joined into one large one, right at the centre of the Mirror. I heard a loud scream, 'Noooooooo!' and then the Mirror disintegrated into thousands of pieces. There was a second of silence and then the sounds of smashed glass echoed through the air as mirror after mirror cracked from the inside and out.

As all trace of the mirrors disappeared from the valley, suddenly a loud cheer resounded in the air as the army began to rejoice. The children ran up to me, jumped up and down in excitement and cried out,

'Abisha! You did it. You're our hero. We love you. ' Each one came up to me and placed a soft, warm kiss on my cheek.

I looked up at the Reachables and saw how they too were undergoing a metamorphoses. First they mutated and took on the form of the hideous Creatures that had terrorised me weeks ago. The transformation continued and their scales began to fall off of them like snakes shedding their skins. Finally they were neither Reachable nor Creature but rather young, innocent and ordinary girls. They gazed around at each other with stunned expressions as if they had just woken from a terrible dream. The girls looked over at me, their heads bowed low and shoulders stooped. One of the girls stepped out from the crowd and in a soft and gentle voice said, 'We are so sorry, please forgive us.'

My heart filled with compassion towards them. They had been trapped just as I had been, but in a different way. 'I forgive you,' I answered tenderly.

My heart lifted and all the tension of the past few weeks seemed to fall off of my shoulders. Could this be the end? Would we see a new time in the valley now, I wondered? I pushed through a crowd of soldiers who were still cheering and congratulating me and I looked out over the town that I had spent my whole life in. The radical change was spectacular.

People started to appear on the streets, coming out of their homes and hidden tunnels underneath the ground. As they began to look at the transformed village, strained expressions and wrinkled brows softened and looks of relief and smiles appeared on all faces. The children of the valley began to run around, laughing and dancing. Mothers wept and fathers took their children up into their arms, swinging them around and around. 'We are free!' I heard them cry. 'The rule of the Mirror is finally over!' It was wonderful to see them so happy and to realise that I had somehow been a part of helping them. The irony of it all hit me as I knew that I, one of the most bound of everyone in Genville had been used to set them free. They still had no idea about the Queen or that she had been the mastermind behind the Mirror, but they would in due time. The Queen, whatever had happened to her? I don't know, all I cared about at that moment was that she was gone.

I sat down on a bench for a moment and tears began to stream down my face. Wiping them away with my hand I looked up and saw Mrs White walking towards me from the bakery. She threw her arms around me and said,

'Thank you, Abisha. I knew that you were special and that one day you would help to set the valley free.' She looked at me pensively and her voice dropped as she asked, 'You've met the Queen, haven't you, child, and heard from your father? We will talk more later but for now I have a party to arrange. It is time to celebrate.'

And then, before I could ask her how she knew about the Queen or me, she took up a loudspeaker and her warm, motherly voice echoed through the air,

'Everyone is welcome to my bakery. Buns are on the house. Bring your family and your friends. In one hour I'll have everything up and running again.'

In union, people let out a loud, 'Yeah!'

A crowd formed, making their way towards Mrs White. Cheers and laughter resounded in the air. The Cave Dwellers started talking to the people of the valley, hugging each other and exchanging stories.

Suddenly I remembered Allister and turned around to look for him. I couldn't see him, he seemed to have vanished. My eyes searched desperately around the area, looking for any glimpse of him. It was more that I could bear to have found him and then to lose him again so quickly. I hadn't even had time to ask him where he had been.

I had almost given up hope when I heard someone call out my name,

'Abisha, Abisha!'

I turned around and saw him standing in front of me. I wanted to cry out but couldn't. I stayed frozen in my place. Fear of being rejected rose up in my heart. What would happen now? Did he feel the way I did? I wanted to run. We had just achieved a great victory together, but in this moment my courage failed me.

I could not bear the thought of him not wanting me. Before my thoughts ran away too far, Allister walked straight towards me and took me into his arms.

'Abisha, I love you,' he declared. 'These past few days when we have been apart have been the worst of my life. I've endured much. Torture, hard training, betrayal. The thought that I might never see you again was beyond what I could bear. Abisha, I love you.'

His words shocked me and my body trembled under the weight of them. I struggled to give a response.

'I, uh, I uh …' My words failed me and I was scared that he would think that I did not care. Miserably I tried to continue,

'I uh, I …' Once again I failed to form words. I had never told anyone that I loved them before and didn't know how. I fell into his arms and wept.

'I don't know if I'm able to love anyone,' I finally confessed. 'Love is not something I know much about. It scares me more than any of the battles we have faced so far. I'm scared to let you down, to not be able to open up my heart.' I was terrified over how he would react. Had I just blown everything with my honesty?

He looked at me for a few seconds, his face serious and intent in thought, and then, just when I thought it was all over, he smiled and said,

'Abisha, love is a journey. There are no experts, no rules that will guarantee success. It is a risk that people take together. I want to take this journey with you.'

His words calmed and comforted me. I figured that if I had been able to learn to love myself over the past few weeks, then surely I would be capable of loving someone else? I took his hand into mine and laughed.

'I guess you are right. I'm willing to take the risk if you are. But I can't promise that I'll do it very well.'

Allister smiled and lifted me up.

'Come Abisha, there are people who want to talk with you and thank you. You've accomplished a great thing today. Many people's lives will never be the same because of it. Hope has been restored to the valley. It was amazing to see you confront the Queen like you did, you showed great courage. Your father would have been so proud of you, if he had been here today. You are truly his daughter, a great warrior.'

We walked slowly towards the bakery to stand in line with the rest of the people. My body ached and I realised that I was hungry. What a relief to be able to eat something in the bakery without any guilt or fear of becoming fat.

The children of the Cave caught up with us and Allister and Mary were reunited with a breathtaking hug. It was obvious that these two really loved each other. I have so much to learn from them.

We spent the rest of the evening with the others at the bakery and the room was full of joy and laughter. I found Sandy in the crowd. We hugged and I asked her to forgive me for not being a good friend. I was afraid how she might react, but she was curious about what I had been through and wanted to know all the details. I promised to tell her everything when I wasn't so tired. I asked her about my aunt and she said that no one knows what had happened to her. Apparently she disappeared the day that I was taken and no one had heard from her since then.

The children of the Cave loved the cakes that Mrs White made and she kept hovering around them like a mother hen with her chicks. She and Ebba liked each other instantly and I'm sure their love of children had something to do with it. The children sang their songs and the people of Genville gathered around them, listening and started singing themselves. A new sound was released across the valley.

It was a wonderful night and as I looked at everyone I suddenly remembered my father's mirror in my pocket and felt an urge to take it out. I opened it up and saw my reflection. I looked tired but happy. Gradually my image melted away and then I saw my father's face again. He was smiling but still trying to tell me something. I drew the mirror closer to me and then I heard these words,

'Abisha, you have won a great victory today. Well done, daughter, you have fought well. Yet, there are still some things that you need to know. I want you to return to the Cave and search through the Glass Room. If you search carefully enough, you will find a silver box. Open it and read the letter inside. I am sorry child, I could not tell you everything at once. You needed to win this battle first.'

I looked over at Allister and he saw the look of shock on my face.

'What is it, Abisha, is everything all right?'

I squeezed his hand reassuringly, answering,

'I'm fine Allister, just tired. We can talk more tomorrow.'

I didn't know what to tell him in that moment. I had so many questions myself.

Evening

I'm in my old bedroom in Genville and it's strange to be here again. I've changed so much since I was here last, learnt so much about myself and my destiny. I know that the words I heard in my dream all those weeks ago are true. I am beautiful and I am special. I know that my life has a purpose.

Dear Diary, we've been on a journey together these past few weeks, and it seems that it is not over yet. Tomorrow, I will return to the Cave and find out what is left for me to discover.

35438896R00132

Printed in Poland
by Amazon Fulfillment
Poland Sp. z o.o., Wrocław